THE GLASS CHILDREN

www.**randomhousechildrens**.co.uk

Kristina Ohlsson

THE GLASS CHILDREN

Translated by Marlaine Delargy

JONATHAN CAPE
LONDON

THE GLASS CHILDREN
A JONATHAN CAPE BOOK 978 0 857 55142 9

First published in Sweden as Glasbarnen by Lilla Piratförlaget
Published in Great Britain by Jonathan Cape,
an imprint of Random House Children's Publishers UK
A Penguin Random House Company

Penguin
Random House
UK

Swedish edition published 2013
This edition published 2014

1 3 5 7 9 10 8 6 4 2

The Random House Group Limited supports the Forest Stewardship Council®
(FSC®), the leading international forest-certification organization. Our
books carrying the FSC label are printed on FSC®-certified paper. FSC is the
only forest-certification scheme supported by the leading environmental
organizations, including Greenpeace. Our paper procurement policy can
be found at www.randomhouse.co.uk/environment.

MIX
Paper from
responsible sources
FSC
www.fsc.org   FSC® C016897

Set in ITC New Baskerville

Random House Children's Publishers UK,
61–63 Uxbridge Road, London W5 5SA

www.**randomhousechildrens**.co.uk
www.**totallyrandombooks**.co.uk
www.**randomhouse**.co.uk

Addresses for companies within The Random House Group Limited
can be found at: www.randomhouse.co.uk/offices.htm

THE RANDOM HOUSE GROUP Limited Reg. No. 954009

A CIP catalogue record for this book is available from the British Library.

Printed and bound in Great Britain by Clays Ltd, St Ives plc

Chapter One

Nobody knew where the family who used to live in the house had gone. One day the previous summer they had simply packed up their things and moved. Since then the house had been standing empty.

'They called me in June,' said the man who was showing Billie and her mum around. 'They said the father had got a new job, and they had to move straight away. Then they asked if I could help them to sell the house.' He shook his head as he led the way up the steps to the front door.

Billie was feeling more and more doubtful

about the whole thing. Were they really going to live here? Her mum turned and smiled at her. It was a new smile that she had adopted when Dad got ill last year. A sad smile that made Billie think of circus clowns.

The man unlocked the front door and went inside. Billie and her mum followed him into the house.

'Of course I couldn't say no when they asked for my help,' the man said. 'I'm no estate agent, but I mean, anyone can sell a house, can't they? However, I didn't have time to deal with the sale when they moved out, and then it was getting towards autumn and winter, so I called them and said it would be best to wait until summer.'

'Have many people been to view the house?' Mum asked.

The man hesitated before he replied. 'Well, not that many, but some. And a number of them were interested.'

Billie thought the man was lying. She was good

at spotting that kind of thing; you could hear it so clearly in people's voices when they weren't telling the truth. Like the time when she asked Mum if Dad was going to die, and Mum said of course he wasn't. Billie had known right away that she was lying.

The man showed them around the house. Upstairs there were two quite small bedrooms with sloping ceilings, while downstairs there was a kitchen, living room, a spare room and a bathroom.

'The kitchen's not very big,' Billie said.

'It's big enough for us,' her mum replied.

Billie looked around. It was an old house. According to the details the man had given them, it had been built almost a hundred years ago. A wooden house, painted blue. The paint was cracked and peeling; she had noticed that while they were standing in the garden.

'They repainted the place just a few years ago,' the man said. 'It used to be yellow.'

3

They were upstairs in one of the bedrooms, and Billie thought the air was difficult to breathe. There was a funny smell in the house, as if no one had lived there for the last twenty years. She didn't care whether it used to be green or yellow or black; she just wanted to get out of there and go home.

Home. To the house in Kristianstad where she had lived for the whole of her twelve-year-old life, the house she never wanted to leave. Mum had got it into her head that they had to move now that there was only her and Billie. To Åhus, a small place about twenty kilometres away where her mum had lived as a child. Billie thought things were just fine. And moving house wasn't going to bring Dad back.

'I like the blue,' her mum said. 'Yellow looks good too, but I can understand why the previous owners chose blue instead. How long did they live here?' she asked as they left the bedroom.

The man was rather evasive. 'I don't really

remember. Three or four years, maybe? As I said, they had to move in a bit of a rush when the mother got a new job.'

'I thought you said it was the father?' Billie said.

The man stared at her and said firmly: 'No, it was the mother.'

The room fell silent, and Billie heard a noise from up above. It sounded as if someone was scampering across the roof tiles.

'Birds,' the man said. 'You get used to it.'

Billie shuddered. This house was unpleasant. Cold and dirty.

And then there was the furniture; the previous owners had left everything behind. Her mum saw her looking, and asked the man when the owners were intending to collect it all.

The man cleared his throat. 'The thing is, if I've understood correctly, the house is being sold together with the furniture,' he said. 'Or not at all.'

Billie's mum was surprised. 'You mean if I don't buy the furniture as well, I can't buy the house?'

'You won't have to pay for the furniture,' the man explained, 'but nobody's going to come along and take it away.'

'I understand,' Mum said, but Billie could see that she didn't understand at all.

Who moved without taking their stuff?

'I'll go and wait in the garden so that you two can have a look round on your own,' the man said, heading off down the stairs.

They heard the front door close, and a moment later they saw him through the window.

'So what do you think?' Mum asked. 'Forget about the furniture; we can get rid of that. And remember we can do the place up however we like.'

Billie had a lump in her throat. It was only just over a year since she had been allowed to redecorate her room at home. Dad had helped her, and they had wondered why he got tired so quickly, and why his back hurt so much.

'I don't want to live in Åhus,' she said. 'I haven't got any friends here; everyone I know lives in town. And I don't like this house.'

'What's wrong with it?' her mum said.

Billie didn't know where to start. Everything was covered in dust, and the windows were filthy. The birds were still running back and forth across the roof, and the walls and floors made funny noises.

'It's just so . . . old,' Billie said eventually.

'But sweetheart, our house in town is old too.'

Billie's eyes were itchy; she rubbed her face with her sleeve.

She didn't like this house, that was all there was to it.

'I'm going downstairs,' her mum said. 'Come down when you've finished looking around.'

The staircase creaked with every step her

mum took, and soon Billie could hear her opening and closing the cupboard doors in the kitchen.

Billie went into the other bedroom, which would be hers if they moved here. It was full of stuff – bookcases and various other pieces of furniture. A bed with a green cover stood against the wall, and in one corner there was a wooden desk that someone had painted pink. On the desk was a pad and some coloured pencils, right next to a pile of drawings. It looked as if someone had been sitting sketching, then simply got up and walked away.

And never came back.

Chapter Two

They moved in four weeks later. Billie couldn't quite get her head round it.

'This is where I want us to live,' her mum said.

And that's what happened.

Because Mum had grown up in Åhus, and insisted that she had always wanted to go back there. Because she wanted them to have a fresh start somewhere different that wasn't too far from Kristianstad.

Billie didn't have the energy to fight, and at least Mum had agreed that she could stay at her school in town, so that she would be with her friends.

'We need to do some cleaning,' Mum said as they were carrying boxes into the house.

Billie couldn't argue with that.

It was July, the middle of the summer holidays, and Billie couldn't remember what she had done with her time since she broke up from school. Her friends seemed to think it was great that she was moving to Åhus. They could come and visit her during the holidays. Cycle to the beach and go swimming. Eat ice cream down by the harbour. Billie had tried to sound just as excited as her friends, but it hadn't really worked. She just kept thinking about all the dust and dirt, and all the things the previous owners had left behind.

It was almost as if they still lived there.

Billie and her mum had been to visit her grandparents in Lund the week before they moved. Grandpa had fired up the barbecue while Grandma boiled new potatoes. They also seemed to think the move to Åhus was a sensible idea.

'Something new will be good for both of you,' Grandma said, stroking Billie's cheek. Then she started to cry, and Grandpa coughed awkwardly and blinked and said the smoke from the barbecue was getting in his eyes. But Billie could see that he was upset too.

Billie had cried so much when Dad died that she didn't think she had any tears left. But she had. They usually came at night, but sometimes it happened in the middle of the day too. No winter or spring had ever been as terrible as this year had been.

They still owned the house in town, but it would soon be up for sale. Billie was hoping that no one would come to see it, and that they would have to move back home. The agent thought it would sell more easily if it was furnished, so Mum had decided they might as well wait before moving their things to the new house.

11

'I mean, there's so much furniture there already, and it's going to take a while to get rid of everything,' she said.

But Billie put her foot down. 'I am not sleeping in their disgusting old beds!' she yelled.

Mum agreed. They would replace the beds, but they would keep everything else.

It was a hot day as they carried everything in. Mum had brought some big cardboard boxes, and Billie put all the stuff that was lying around in her room in one of them. She cleared the pink desk, carefully picking up the drawings that had been left out. She wasn't sure, but she thought they had been done by a girl. Most of them were black and white; only a few had been coloured in.

The pictures were of different things.

A big cat, sitting on a rock.

A lot of trees; Billie thought they were meant to represent a forest. A boy was peering out from behind one of the trunks.

Another picture showed a girl who looked really cross.

Billie put them right at the bottom of the box and covered them up with other bits and pieces. She didn't like the fact that the other family had left such obvious signs of their existence. Mum kept saying they needed a fresh start, but how could anything feel new or fresh in such an old house?

Mum appeared in the doorway. 'I'm going shopping; do you want to come?'

Billie thought for a moment. No, she didn't want to go shopping.

'OK,' Mum said. 'I won't be long.'

So Billie was alone in the new house for the first time.

Chapter Three

When Mum had gone, the house was completely silent. Billie put the last of the things she wanted to get rid of in a box, and went downstairs to fetch the vacuum cleaner. Mum had left the front door open, and Billie hurried over and pushed it shut. She locked it too.

As the door closed she heard a window banging in one of the rooms. She tiptoed into the living room, but none of the windows were open. Billie stood completely still, listening carefully. The noise continued, but it was coming from somewhere else.

Then she saw something that made her forget the banging for a moment.

The ceiling light in the living room.

It was moving. It was slowly swinging to and fro, like the pendulum of an old clock.

It must be the draught from the window, Billie thought. But all the windows in the living room were closed. So how could the light be swinging to and fro?

She went into the spare room. The floor was virtually covered with boxes and assorted junk. Billie was relieved to see that the window was wide open; she quickly closed it. She felt the same as she did about the front door; she didn't dare leave it open. Nor could she bring herself to go back and look at the light in the living room. What if it was still moving?

Billie found the vacuum cleaner in a corner by the door. She wondered whether she had ever experienced a more peculiar summer holiday. A summer holiday filled with moving house and cleaning. A summer holiday without Dad. She forced herself to take a deep breath.

As Billie picked up the vacuum cleaner, she caught sight of a little table. It was low, like a coffee table, but much smaller. She wondered what it was for; perhaps it was the kind of thing Grandma put a plant on?

The table was covered in dust, but Billie could see that it was brightly coloured. It had metal legs, and the top was made up of small, shiny tiles in blue, red and gold. Cautiously she drew a line in the dust with her finger, and saw how the tiles glowed. This was the first beautiful thing she had seen in the house. She would ask her mum if she could have it in her room.

As she carried the vacuum cleaner upstairs, she thought about the light, swinging from its hook on the ceiling. It must have been the draught from the spare room that had made it move. What else could it have been?

* * *

The sun slowly disappeared behind the tall pine trees on the other side of the road opposite their house. Billie and her mum were sitting on the patio eating spaghetti Bolognese.

'Do you fancy cycling down to the sea for an evening dip?' Mum said, her eyes sparkling. 'I think we've earned it after all our hard work.'

A bike ride and an evening swim. It sounded wonderful. Billie finished her glass of milk and they set off.

'What do you think happened to the family who used to live here?' Billie said when they had been cycling along in companionable silence for a while.

'What do you mean, *happened*?' Mum said.

'I don't really know, but don't you think it's odd that they just cleared off and left so much behind?'

'I suppose so,' Mum said. 'It is a bit strange that they just left. But that's what happens sometimes; things can change very quickly.'

They didn't say anything else until they reached the shore.

The water was blue and cold. There wasn't a breath of wind to create ripples on the shining surface. Billie stopped when the water swirled around her knees, but her mum kept on going and ran until it reached her waist. Then she threw herself forward and disappeared into the blue. A few seconds later she bobbed up again.

'It's fantastic!' she shouted. 'Come on, Billie!'

Billie ran towards her mum. She had forgotten that the water in Åhus was always too cold – and that it was so shallow. Grandpa used to say that it was so shallow you could walk all the way to Poland.

The beach was narrow but long. In the distance to the right it was just possible to make out the pier at the inlet to the harbour. Billie was planning to cycle down to the harbour as soon as she had time. It was a lovely place to sit and read.

18

She spotted him when she had finished her swim and was rolling up her towel. A boy with dark hair and brown eyes. He was sitting on the sand not far away, wearing red shorts and nothing else. Why was he staring at them?

Billie's mum came out of the water, shaking her hair. She must have followed Billie's gaze, because she said: 'He looks nice.'

Billie could feel herself blushing. Why did parents always think it was OK to say that kind of stuff? *Nice.* Was that really the right thing to say about a kid?

'No, he doesn't,' Billie said. 'He looks stupid, sitting there staring at us.'

She glared angrily at the boy, who slowly turned away. But when Billie and her mum walked past him a little while later, he was gazing at them again. Billie straightened her back and made a point of looking in the other direction. She had a feeling that the boy kept on watching them until they reached their bikes and rode off.

* * *

It was dusk by the time they got back to the house. Mum took the towels and went to hang them on the clothes line next to the woodshed in the back garden.

'You go inside; I'll be there in a minute,' she said.

Billie quickly walked around the house and onto the patio. The pine trees on the other side of the road loomed tall and dark. There were lights on in several of the other houses, but they all had big gardens, and it didn't feel as if any of them were particularly close. A squirrel that must have been hiding on the patio scampered down the steps, giving Billie a fright.

She thought about the boy on the beach, and her hand was shaking slightly as she took the key out of her pocket and unlocked the front door. She stepped inside and closed the door behind her. She still had sand on her feet, and she brushed it off with her hands. Tiny grains of yellow sand rained down on the rug.

The ceiling light in the hallway flickered when she switched it on. She remembered the little table; perhaps she could clean it up and take it to her room right away?

The spare room had only a small wall light; its muted glow coloured the room yellow. Billie went over to the little table and bent down to pick it up. Suddenly she stiffened. That was impossible. She crouched down so that she could get a closer look. But no, her eyes weren't deceiving her. And the more she stared at the dusty surface of the table, the more frightened she became.

Above the line that she herself had drawn in the dust, someone had left the print of a very small hand. It was as if a child had come into the house while they were at the beach, pressed its hand in the dust, then walked away.

Chapter Four

However hard she tried, Billie couldn't stop thinking about that handprint in the dust. Someone had been in their house while they were away. But her mum didn't believe her. She said that Billie must have made the print herself.

'But that's impossible!' Billie had said, placing her own hand over the print. 'My hand is much bigger!' She couldn't understand how her mum could think that she was lying.

'So what are you saying? That a small child sneaked into our house?'

Billie didn't know what to think, so she didn't

answer. But she was scared. She found it difficult to get to sleep, and during the night she was woken by the birds running around on the roof, and by the strange creaking from the walls and floors.

'That's just the way it is with old houses,' her mum said. 'They make noises.'

But Billie didn't feel safe, and the sense that things weren't right began to grow. Sometimes she imagined that they weren't alone in the house.

She hoped she would feel better when they had been living there for a while. She was too old to believe in ghosts, and of course her mum was right when she said it was impossible for a small child to have come into their house while they were out. But in that case, how had the handprint got there?

It started to rain. Billie spent most of the time in her room, lying on her bed and reading as the raindrops hammered on the roof. After five days of uninterrupted bad weather, Mum announced that she had more or less finished sorting out the house, and at the same time the sun reappeared.

'I thought we were going to get rid of all the stuff we put in boxes?' Billie said as they put the last bits and pieces in the spare room.

'Yes, but the weather has been so terrible,' her mum said. 'And you remember Martin, the man who showed us round? He's promised to take care of it all if I just leave it here.'

Billie remembered the man, and she also remembered that she had disliked him as much as she disliked the house. So his name was Martin, was it?

'He told a whole load of lies,' she said.

'Oh, Billie,' her mum said. She looked tired.

'But he did,' Billie insisted. 'He said the family who used to live here had moved because the father got a new job, then all of a sudden he said it was the mother.'

24

'He probably forgot,' her mum said. 'Just let it go.'

But Billie thought again about the handprint in the dust, and she couldn't understand why her mum wasn't frightened by what had happened.

The best thing about Åhus was that it was so small. Nothing was far away, and you could get everywhere by bike. Billie got into the habit of trying to go somewhere every day.

A place she particularly liked to visit was the library, which was behind the large supermarket by the harbour. Billie loved books. She had even decided not to pack away the books that the previous family had left in her room, but to leave them in the bookcase.

The librarian recognized Billie by this stage, and greeted her with a smile as she walked up to the desk to ask about a book she had ordered.

'You're in luck,' the librarian said cheerfully. 'It's just come in!'

She turned and took a book off the shelf behind her. The book was thick, with brown covers, and there was a rubber band around it to secure a piece of paper with Billie's name and address on it.

'There you go,' said the librarian, removing the rubber band.

Billie took out her library card. As she handed it to the librarian, she brushed against the piece of paper and it drifted onto the floor. Just as she was about to bend down to retrieve it, she heard a voice:

'I'll get it for you.'

Billie gave a start; she hadn't noticed that there was someone behind her. An elderly lady picked up the piece of paper and read it before handing it to Billie.

The lady was very small, even shorter than Billie. And she was wearing such strange clothes: a long dress that looked as old as she was. She smelled funny too – like candle wax. Billie could tell from the librarian's expression that she recognized the old lady, and she didn't look pleased.

'Ella, your book still hasn't arrived,' she said sharply. It was as if she thought the old lady visited the library too often, and as if she didn't like her.

'Oh well,' said Ella. 'In that case I'll have to come back another day.'

'I've already said that we'll ring you when it comes in.'

The old lady didn't speak for a moment, then she said: 'There's no need. I haven't got much to do; I'm happy to call in.'

Then she turned to Billie. 'I noticed from the piece of paper that you live on Sparrisvägen,' she said. 'You haven't moved into the blue house opposite the pine trees, have you?'

Her voice was friendly, but her expression was anxious. Billie felt uncomfortable. Why was the lady interested in where she lived?

'Yes, we have,' she said eventually. 'But we haven't been there for long.'

Ella shook her head, and Billie thought she looked upset.

'I was sure nobody else would move in there,' she said.

The librarian gave Billie her book and card.

'Thanks,' Billie said automatically.

'You're welcome. Now you get off home before Ella fills your head with gossip.'

Ella was annoyed. 'I haven't said anything!' she insisted loudly.

'No, and you're not going to,' the librarian said. 'I'm sure this young lady is very happy in her new house, and she really doesn't need to hear your fairy tales.'

Ella snorted. 'Fairy tales,' she said crossly. 'I don't think so! They're just as true as I'm standing here now.'

What are they talking about? Billie wondered. She clutched the book to her chest.

'Is there something the matter with our house?' she said, trying to sound confident.

She failed; her voice was unsteady, and came out more like a whisper.

'Not at all,' the librarian said. 'It's just Ella, imagining things.'

What kind of things? Billie wanted to ask. But she didn't. Something held her curiosity in check, as if she was afraid of what she might hear.

'I'm not imagining anything,' Ella snapped. 'But don't worry, I won't bother you any longer.'

She swept out of the library, her skirts rustling as she went.

'You'd better wait here for a few minutes to make sure she's gone,' the librarian said to Billie, who couldn't shake off the feeling that Ella had been trying to tell her something; something important.

'What did you mean by gossip?' she asked tentatively.

'Nothing for you to worry about,' the librarian

said. 'It's just Ella, talking nonsense. Various different families have lived in your house over the past few years, and that seems to have fired up Ella's imagination.'

Billie stood there by the desk, clutching her book. She wondered what it was that Ella had wanted to tell her. And she wondered how come their address was so well known that both Ella and the librarian recognized it?

'I have to go home,' she mumbled.

Without really knowing why, she ran out of the library and over to her bike. Ella wasn't waiting for her. She dropped the key no less than twice as she tried to undo the lock.

There was something wrong with their house. Just as Billie had known all along.

Chapter Five

'Isn't it time you invited a friend over?' Billie's mum said when they were lying on the beach a day or so later. 'You only see your friends when we're in Kristianstad.'

Billie had been thinking the same thing herself. It probably was time. Her friends in town kept on asking if they could come and see her.

'I might ask Simona,' she said.

'Sounds like a good idea,' her mum said.

She looked at Billie through her sunglasses and gave her a gentle nudge. 'Isn't that the boy we saw when we came down for a swim the first evening?' she said.

She nodded towards a dark-haired boy who was sitting on the sand a short distance away. Billie recognized him at once. He was wearing the same red shorts, and he didn't appear to have a beach towel with him this time either.

'Why is he just sitting there staring?' Billie said; she could hear how bad-tempered she sounded.

'Perhaps he's bored,' her mum said. 'Why don't you go over and talk to him?'

It was just typical of her mum to come up with something so stupid. *Why don't you go over and talk to him?* You just didn't do that kind of thing; everybody knew that.

'No chance,' she said.

Her mum got up and brushed the sand off her legs. 'Coming for a swim?'

Billie looked down at the book she was reading. 'The water's too cold.'

'Please yourself,' her mum said, taking off her glasses. 'Keep an eye on my stuff, will you?'

Then she turned and ran into the sea.

Billie stayed where she was, sitting on the towel with the book on her lap. It was the book she had collected from the library when the old lady called Ella had been there. She was still curious. Billie had tried to talk to her mum about what she had heard, but her mum had merely said that she shouldn't listen to gossip.

But how could Mum be so sure that it was just gossip? Billie was desperate to know what Ella had wanted to tell her. The question was, how could she track her down? It seemed as if she visited the library quite often; perhaps she would be there the next time Billie went.

A cloud drifted across the sun, and Billie shivered. Her mum had been right; she ought to ask a friend over. She needed someone to talk to, someone who would listen.

Billie stole a glance at the boy in the red shorts.

He caught her eye and smiled. Billie immediately turned away. What was he up to?

A little while later, Billie couldn't help looking in his direction once more. But by then he had disappeared.

The bus from Kristianstad stopped at Vatten-tornsområdet, and Billie was waiting when it arrived. Simona had been delighted when Billie rang to invite her. She decided to come that very same day.

Happiness made Billie feel warm all over. Why hadn't she asked a friend over before now?

The bus driver helped Simona get her bike out of the storage hold. 'You take care now,' he said.

Billie and Simona giggled as they put on their helmets. Billie pointed things out as they cycled the short distance from the bus stop to Sparrisvägen. She showed Simona the old clog factory; according to her mum, she and her brother used to steal clogs from there when they were kids. Billie also showed Simona in which direction the sea lay.

'I'd like to move too,' Simona said. 'Just make a fresh start!' And she laughed out loud.

They could smell cooking as they cycled up the garden path. Billie's mum had set up the barbecue on the patio, and waved cheerfully as they whizzed past her. She was wearing the blue apron Dad used to wear when he was barbecuing, and her sunglasses were pushed up on top of her head. Billie had always wished she had lovely curls like her mum, but instead she had inherited Dad's fair, straight hair.

'This is lovely! And you've got all this old furniture!' Simona said as Billie showed her around the house.

'It's not ours,' Billie explained. 'The people who used to live here left loads of things behind.'

'How come?' Simona's red hair stood out like a halo.

Billie didn't answer; instead, she took Simona

by the hand. 'Come on, I'll show you my room.'

She led her friend up the stairs.

'Cool!' Simona said, looking around. 'And you've got a sloping ceiling! I've always wanted one of those.'

She sat down on Billie's bed; Billie could see that the bookcase had caught her eye.

'Are those your books?' she asked.

'No, mine are still at our old house in town. These belonged to the girl who had this room before me.'

Billie stopped short. She had said 'the girl'. It was as if she knew for sure that this had been a girl's room, but of course she didn't. She had just made that assumption.

Simona got up and walked over to the bookcase. 'They're beautiful, but they're really old,' she said, running her hand over the spines.

The same thing had occurred to Billie. She had flicked through some of them and thought they were probably children's books, but she had never heard of any of them.

'Is the family who used to live here still in Åhus, or did they move away?' Simona asked, taking out one of the books.

'Nobody knows where they went,' Billie said, lowering her voice so that her mum wouldn't hear.

Simona replaced the book. 'But they can't just have vanished,' she said.

Billie swallowed. 'That's the way it seems.' She hesitated, then added: 'I think there's something wrong with this house. And that's why they didn't want to stay here.'

Åhus was bathed in evening sunlight as Billie and Simona cycled down to the harbour. Mum had said she was going to watch something on TV, but gave them money for ice creams.

The gravel crunched beneath their wheels as Billie took them on a short cut. They passed the disused Åhus park where her mum had gone to discos when she was younger, and Jocke's old bike shop, where Dad had bought Billie her very first bicycle.

They parked their bikes in front of the old fortress in the harbour and went on board the Ice Cream Boat. They had enough money for a big cone each – two scoops topped with whipped cream. Simona found a table by the rail.

Her face was a picture of concentration as she started on her ice cream.

'So you think the house is haunted?'

Billie nearly choked. 'No, no,' she said. 'Not haunted.'

Because there was no such thing as ghosts. Or was there?

'But what about that handprint you mentioned?' Simona said. 'How did that get there while you were out?'

'I don't know,' Billie said.

And then she suddenly saw the boy in the red

shorts, the boy she had seen on the beach. He was sitting on the edge of the quay, watching them. And this time it didn't look as if he was intending to leave them alone.

 # Chapter Six

It was Simona who suggested that they should go over and speak to him.

'We need to find out what he wants, if he keeps on turning up like this,' she said.

Everything seemed so straightforward to Simona, although Billie knew that things had been difficult for her in the past. Her mother had been badly hurt in a car accident, and had had to learn to walk again. Billie couldn't remember ever having seen Simona cry at the time – not even once.

When they left the Ice Cream Boat, the boy

was sitting on a bench, waiting for them. He stood up as they reached him. 'Hi,' he said with a smile.

Billie reluctantly admitted to herself that he looked pretty good.

She and Simona both said hi.

'Did you want something?' Billie said. 'Only you keep following me around.'

The boy looked surprised. 'No, I don't,' he said. 'You keep turning up wherever I am. I'm the one who should be asking what you want.'

Billie was so taken aback that she didn't know what to say. She certainly wasn't chasing him – quite the reverse.

'Maybe it's just an accident that you two keep on bumping into one another,' Simona suggested.

Typical – she always came up with the right thing to say.

'Maybe,' the boy said. 'In which case it's what I'd call a happy accident.'

He held out his hand to say hello properly, the way adults do. 'Aladdin,' he said. 'Nice to meet you!'

Billie couldn't help giggling. Nobody their age said 'Nice to meet you'! She didn't want to upset him, so she quickly shook his hand and said: 'Billie. And this is my friend Simona.'

'Billy? Isn't that a boy's name?'

'Billie with an *i-e* at the end – that makes it a girl's name.'

'Aha,' said the boy, bowing politely. 'In that case, Billie with an *i-e* at the end, may I show you and your friend around the harbour?'

His name really *was* Aladdin, and he came from Turkey. However, he didn't really remember anything about it; his parents had moved to Sweden when Aladdin was just two years old.

'We've got family here,' he said as they walked along past the neat rows of boats. 'Dad thought he'd get rich if he came over here and cooked Turkish food for the Swedes.'

'What kind of food is that?' Simona asked.

'Kebabs, grilled meat, that kind of thing,' Aladdin said. 'Now he's got his own restaurant.'

'Does your dad own the Turk in the Tower?' Billie asked in amazement.

'Yep,' Aladdin said, bursting with pride.

The Turk in the Tower was the best restaurant in Åhus. It was right at the top of an old disused water tower.

'Have you ever eaten there?' Aladdin asked.

'Only once,' Billie replied.

'Twice,' Simona said. 'Once on my dad's fortieth birthday, and once when my brother passed his driving test.'

A dad and a brother. Billie had neither, and fell silent.

'This is where I live with my parents,' Aladdin said. He was pointing to a large houseboat moored at the quayside. Billie thought it looked like a shoebox.

'Here?' She couldn't hide her surprise.

'Yep – well, in the summer anyway. In the winter we live in a house next door to the restaurant.'

'That's brilliant!' Simona exclaimed. 'The houseboat, I mean.'

What an exciting life Aladdin seemed to have. Parents who owned a restaurant, and a houseboat in the harbour. Billie felt a sudden stab of envy. Why did she have to live in a horrible old haunted house?

'We ought to be getting back,' she said.

'Call round any time,' Aladdin said. 'I'm nearly always here.'

He was smiling as he spoke. In fact, he smiled practically all the time. Billie couldn't help smiling back. Maybe it would be easier to live in Åhus if she at least had a friend.

They made up a bed for Simona on a mattress in Billie's room. Her mum sorted out sheets and a towel, and asked them several times if there was anything else they needed. Both Simona and Billie shook their heads and said no, they were fine. When Billie's mum had said goodnight and closed the door, they lay awake talking for a while. They chatted about their friends in town, and what it would be like when they moved up a year in the autumn. Simona said that she and her parents were going on holiday to Gotland, and Billie told her that Mum had decided they would be spending the whole summer in Åhus.

As they turned out the light and settled down to go to sleep, Billie thought about the books in the bookcase in her room. The previous family had left a lot of things behind, but it was the books that bothered Billie the most. Who moved house without taking their books with them?

Chapter Seven

At first Billie couldn't work out what had woken her. The house was completely silent. She couldn't even hear the birds that were usually running about on the roof. She curled up under the covers, listening hard.

Then she heard Simona moving in her bed.

'Are you asleep?' Simone whispered.

'No,' Billie whispered back. 'Did you hear something?'

She saw the dark shape of Simona getting up from the mattress.

'It sounded as if someone was tapping on the window.'

Her voice was so faint that Billie could only just make out what she said.

'But that's impossible,' she hissed back. 'Nobody's tall enough to tap on a first-floor window!'

Then the sound came again.

Simona was right. It sounded as if someone was tapping on the window above Billie's bed. Cautious, gentle little taps.

Billie was so scared that she was almost in tears. 'We've got to go and get Mum,' she whispered.

'Ssh!' Simona said.

Perhaps it was only a bird. Billie hardly even dared glance at the window, in spite of the fact that the white roller-blind her mum had put up was pulled right down. What if someone was standing outside? On a ladder?

Simona tiptoed over to the window.

'Be careful!' Billie said.

The tapping suddenly stopped.

Both Billie and Simona froze. They waited for several minutes for the tapping to resume, but it didn't happen. Simona walked slowly over to the window and pulled the blind away, just an inch or two. She peeped out through the gap.

'Nothing,' she said.

It was pitch dark outside. It was well after midnight, so none of the neighbours were likely to be up and about. All the houses were silent and in darkness.

Simona tugged at the bottom of the blind and it flew up with a loud crack that made both girls jump. They were already on edge, and immediately got the giggles.

'We'll wake Mum if we carry on like this,' Billie said, burying her head in the pillow to stop herself from laughing.

Simona was looking out of the window again, and Billie went over to join her. At first she couldn't see a thing, but eventually her eyes got used to the darkness, and she was able to make out the trees in the garden and the outline of the neighbour's house a short distance away.

'It must have been a bird,' Simona said firmly. 'Nobody could reach this high up.'

Billie pulled down the blind. 'It was definitely a bird,' she echoed. 'Let's go back to bed.'

Her heart beat a little slower each time she said 'bird'. Of course it was a bird. What else could it have been?

'I need the loo,' Simona said, just as Billie got into bed.

'I'll come downstairs with you,' Billie said, throwing back the covers.

She couldn't let her friend go wandering around the house all on her own after what had just happened.

She opened the door very slowly so that it wouldn't creak and wake her mum. Simona tiptoed down the stairs with Billie right behind her. She might as well go to the loo as well.

Simona went in and closed the door, while Billie waited in the hallway. She didn't dare go anywhere else. The house was full of sounds, odd little clicks and creaks everywhere, as if the house was growing and in pain. She wouldn't mind betting that it wasn't like this on board Aladdin's houseboat. Billie imagined he would be able to hear the water lapping against the side of the boat; what a lovely sound to fall asleep to. If they became friends, she and Aladdin, perhaps Billie and Simona would be able to have a sleepover on the houseboat one day.

Then Billie heard the tapping noise again. It was just the same as before, almost like a whisper, but it was very clear. Billie's heart was racing. If only Simona would get a move on!

It sounded as if the tapping was coming from the room beyond the kitchen – the spare room. Billie listened and thought about the little handprint in the dust on the table. That same little hand was tapping on the window right now, she was sure of it.

Simona flushed the loo and opened the door.

'Can you hear it?' Billie whispered before Simona had time to speak.

Simona listened hard, frowning. 'No – what am I supposed to be hearing?'

Simona was right – there wasn't a sound now.

'It was just like the tapping we heard upstairs,' Billie said.

They listened again.

But the sound had gone.

'That's weird,' Simona said. 'Where was it coming from this time?'

'From the spare room.'

They looked at one another, then they crept along to the spare room and peeped inside. They stood in the doorway. Everything looked just the same as usual – boxes piled on top of one another, and pieces of furniture they had no use for. The table that Billie had liked so much was still standing in the corner. She didn't want it any more.

'Where did you find that handprint?' Simona asked.

'There,' Billie said, pointing.

The room was dark, but they hadn't got round to putting up any curtains yet. Simona went to the window and peered out, with Billie close behind her. Everything was quiet, and there wasn't a soul in sight. Simona turned and went over to the table instead.

'What's this comic?' she said.

Billie bent down to have a look. It was difficult to see in the gloom, but it didn't matter, because Billie recognized it right away. On the table where she had found the handprint, someone had placed the old comic that Billie had packed away in a box on the very first day when they moved in.

It looked as if someone had written something

on it. Billie's heart was pounding so hard that she thought it might burst as she leaned closer and read the childish handwriting:

GO AWAY!

Chapter Eight

Under normal circumstances Mum hardly ever got cross, but this time she was furious.

'Do you think I don't realize you wrote *GO AWAY!* on that comic yourself?' she snapped the following morning when Billie made another attempt to talk to her about everything that had gone on during the night.

'Ask Simona if you don't believe me!' Billie yelled back. 'Or ask yourself! I mean, you've seen the comic!'

'There's no point. You could have written on it while Simona was in the loo.'

How could she think that Billie would lie about something like this? Billie was so angry she thought she might actually explode. Simona sat in silence at the breakfast table, watching them argue.

Billie's mum had been very cross when they woke her up during the night to tell her about the tapping and the comic. She said that if Billie and Simona couldn't behave themselves when they were sharing a room, then there would be no more sleepovers.

'You always spoil things!' Billie had shouted after her as she headed back up to her room after telling them to get to bed at once.

Mum had turned round and shot down the stairs so fast that Billie had thought she might fall.

'Am I really the one who spoils things?' she had said, her voice icily calm. 'You're the one who spoils things, Billie. All the time. Be honest – you don't like the fact that we've moved to Åhus, and you're doing your best to make sure we move back to town.'

Billie hadn't known what to say. To be fair, her mother was right. She hated living here, but she would never have come up with something like this. Never in a million years.

'I make the decisions in this house, Billie,' her mother had continued in the same calm tone of voice. 'Because I am the adult, not you. You're not the only one who misses Dad and wishes things could go back to the way they were. I feel exactly the same.'

She paused, looking as if she was about to cry.

'But it's just not possible,' she said after a moment. 'That's not the way things work. This is how life is now, and we just have to make the best of the situation. And the best thing for us was to move out of town and start afresh somewhere else.'

With those words she had left Simona and Billie standing in the hallway and gone up to bed. Billie had hardly slept a wink for the rest of the night, and at breakfast the quarrel had started up again.

'I can't talk about this any more,' her mum said, getting to her feet. She started clearing the table.

'What are you going to do today?' she asked.

Billie looked at Simona, then up at the sky. It was cloudy, but it wasn't raining.

'How about cycling to the library?' she suggested.

Mum sighed when she heard Billie mention the library, but Simona nodded. Billie was pleased, because she really wanted to see that old lady again.

'Good idea,' Simona said. 'Maybe we could go down to the harbour as well? We could call on Aladdin.'

'Aladdin?' Mum said, looking at Billie. 'Who's Aladdin?'

'A boy who lives on a boat in the harbour. His parents own the Turk in the Tower.'

'And you know him, do you?'

Billie shrugged, trying to look as if she wasn't remotely impressed by either the houseboat or the restaurant. 'Sort of,' she said.

Her mum smiled for the first time that morning. 'Is he the boy in the red shorts?'

'Maybe.'

Before Billie had time to defend herself, Mum had thrown her arms around her.

'Oh, you've made a friend! I'm so pleased!'

Billie wriggled free of her mum's bear hug. 'I don't know if I'd call him a friend.'

She had to get her mother to calm down. If she got the idea that Billie and Aladdin were friends, she would never agree to move back into town.

'Off you go, girls,' her mum said. 'I'll finish up here.'

Billie and Simona went up to Billie's room.

'Shouldn't I have mentioned Aladdin?' Simona said.

'It's OK – I just don't want Mum to get the idea that I like living here.'

Simona stroked her arm. 'Do you really miss Kristianstad?'

'All the time,' Billie whispered.

A big fat fly was buzzing around up by the ceiling. It was flying back and forth, faster and faster. As if it was trapped and frightened.

Like me, Billie thought. She had begun to think of the house as a prison. *Neither of us can escape from here*.

It felt good to get out. Simona suggested that they should cycle along the track leading to the village through the pine trees. Billie had always loved spending time in the forest, and was happy to agree. The wind was sighing in the tall treetops, and the ground was covered in a thick carpet of brown, fallen needles. A small meadow opened out on the far side of the pine copse.

Billie thought about what had happened

during the night. They definitely hadn't imagined the sound of tapping on the windows. And then there was the comic. Who had put it on the table? Who could get into the house?

'You believe me, don't you?' Billie said to Simona when they started to discuss what they had experienced.

'Of course I do!' Simona said. 'But I think it's really creepy!'

Billie thought so too. 'Do you believe in ghosts?' she said.

'I don't know,' Simona replied. 'Sometimes when I go to stay with Grandpa I imagine I can hear Grandma's footsteps in the hallway at night.'

Billie's eyes widened. 'You're joking,' she said, thinking about all the times she thought she had heard her dad in their house in town.

'She had a particular way of walking,' Simona said. 'And I can hear it when I stay over at Grandpa's. But it's fine.'

'Fine?' Billie was taken aback.

'Yes,' Simona said. 'It's fine. Because I think it's good for Grandpa that she's there. That she's kind of, like, watching over him.'

'Like an imaginary friend?' Billie said.

'Something like that,' Simona said. 'Only for real.'

Chapter Nine

They found Aladdin sitting on the jetty by the houseboat, fiddling with some bits of plastic. His face lit up when he saw them.

'Hi there!' he said, waving to the two girls.

'Hi,' Billie said. 'What are you doing?'

'Building a model plane.'

'It's very small,' Simona said.

'Mum says I can only build small planes, because I make so many of them,' Aladdin explained.

He looked at the books under Billie's arm. 'Have you been to the library?'

Billie nodded, and slipped the books into the shopping bag Mum had given her. The old lady hadn't been at the library, but hopefully she would be there another day.

'Do you like reading too?' Simona asked Aladdin.

'Not really – I'm more into building stuff.'

He got to his feet. 'Would you like to have a look around?'

It was the cosiest home Billie had ever been in. All the walls were painted white, and small green plants adorned every window. Blue curtains in the hallway, pink in the kitchen. A blue kitchen table and chairs of different colours.

'Fantastic pictures,' Simona said, referring to the pictures in the kitchen that showed people dancing.

'Mum paints,' Aladdin said.

He took them downstairs and into a bedroom with a double bed. The room must be underwater, because the windows were small, round portholes just below the ceiling.

'Mum and Dad's room,' Aladdin said.

'Where do you sleep?' Simona wanted to know.

A cunning expression came into Aladdin's eyes. 'Up top,' he said.

They went back to the kitchen, and Aladdin unfolded a ladder that was fixed to the ceiling. He climbed up and opened a hatch. Billie and Simona watched as he disappeared through the hole, waving to them to follow him.

'Wow!' Billie said as she poked her head into Aladdin's room.

When you looked at the boat from the outside, it looked like a big box with a smaller box on top. Aladdin lived in the smaller box. He had a window on every side, and the room was so small that there was only space for a bed, a bedside table, and a lamp.

'This is to die for,' Simona said when she

64

arrived. 'I've always thought I'd like to live in a lighthouse when I grow up, but this is really cool too.'

Aladdin threw himself on the bed. 'Good, isn't it?'

That was the least you could say. It was like his very own castle, where the only way in was through a hole in the floor.

Billie looked around. You could see the entire harbour from Aladdin's windows.

'Haven't you got any curtains?' Simona asked.

'No – I like to keep an eye on things,' Aladdin said.

Billie thought about Aladdin, sleeping alone in his box, with his parents two floors below, beneath the surface of the water. 'Don't you get scared when it's dark?' she said.

Aladdin looked completely bewildered. 'I've never understood that,' he said. 'What is there to be afraid of when it's dark that isn't out there when it's light?'

Billie and Simona looked at one another. They were both thinking exactly the same thing.

Simona sat down on the floor. 'Billie's house is haunted,' she said.

Billie sat down too. 'Or else someone is coming into the house whenever they feel like it and doing weird things.'

She explained what had happened since she and her mum had moved in.

Aladdin let out a low whistle. 'Now I understand,' he said. 'So you and your mum must be living in the Scary House.'

'Sorry?' Billie said, feeling stupid.

'The Scary House. Something bad has happened to everybody who's moved in there,' Aladdin said. 'Although I'm sure it's just a coincidence. I mean, there's no such thing as ghosts.'

'Why is it called the Scary House?' Simona asked.

'Because it's so scary that you shake with fear

when you walk in,' Aladdin said, laughing. 'Stupid, or what?'

Billie thought it was embarrassing rather than stupid. Obviously their house was well known throughout the village; it even had a ridiculous nickname.

Aladdin realized what she was thinking. 'It's only at my school that it's called the Scary House,' he said.

Good, Billie thought. *I'm definitely not going there, then.*

After a short silence, Aladdin said: 'Actually, my mum believes in spirits and ghosts and all that kind of stuff.'

It started to rain, the heavy drops pattering on the roof of Aladdin's room. The wind was making the boat rock slightly.

'Why?' Billie said, wrapping her arms around her knees.

'She says she can talk to them,' Aladdin said. 'She says that many of the dead are very angry, and want to come back to life. But of course they can't.'

'So what do they do when they're angry?' Simona said.

'That's when they start messing with those of us who are still alive.'

Aladdin pondered for a while, then asked: 'So do you two believe in all that stuff?'

Billie thought about it. What other explanation could there be for the handprint in the dust and the tapping on the window? She couldn't decide which was worse – a ghost, or a person playing tricks on them.

'I don't know what I believe,' she said. 'But I do know that something's not right about the house where I live.'

They sat in silence for a long time, listening to the rain. Billie thought about what Aladdin had said – according to his mother, some of the dead were angry because they were no longer alive. What if there was an angry ghost in their house? How could she and her mum get rid of it?

When the rain stopped, Billie and Simona decided to carry on down to the supermarket to get some shopping for Billie's mum. Aladdin wanted to go with them. Before getting off the boat and locking up, he slipped into a cupboard in the hallway and emerged carrying a unicycle.

'Can you ride that?' Billie asked.

'Of course I can – it's a piece of cake,' Aladdin said.

Billie and Simona watched in fascination as he leaped onto the cycle and shot away. Everything seemed to be so easy for Aladdin, just as it was for Simona.

The supermarket was quite big. Aladdin and Simona messed about by the freezers while Billie collected all the things on the list Mum had given her.

As she was choosing some bananas, she felt a hand on her shoulder. She assumed it was

Aladdin or Simona, so she picked up one of the bananas and swung around, holding it in front of her like a gun. 'Hands up!' she said.

Behind her stood Ella, the lady from the library.

Billie was so shocked that she dropped the banana. 'Oh, sorry,' she said automatically.

But Ella didn't seem to have noticed that she had just been in mortal danger from a banana. 'I need to talk to you,' she hissed. 'Very soon.'

Billie looked over her shoulder, wondering where Aladdin and Simona had got to. 'Right,' she said.

'It's important,' the old lady whispered. 'You and your family could be in great danger. It's to do with the house.'

Wasn't that exactly what Aladdin had heard at school – that it was an unlucky house?

'My name is Ella Bengtsson,' the old lady said. 'I live on Snickarhaksvägen in Äspet.'

Äspet was the area on the other side of the

harbour, that much Billie knew. But where on earth were Simona and Aladdin? Billie was beginning to feel slightly panicky, standing here on her own with the whispering old lady who smelled so peculiar.

'Promise you'll come,' Ella whispered.

'I promise,' Billie said in a small voice.

'Good,' the old lady replied.

Then she picked up her basket of groceries and disappeared.

Chapter Ten

Billie and Simona managed to cycle over to Äspet twice to look for Ella before Simona had to go home, but they didn't find her.

'You have to carry on looking,' Simona said as they were saying goodbye at the bus stop. 'I'll come over and help you again soon.'

Billie nodded. She felt it was important to find out why someone had crept into their house and written *GO AWAY!* on an old comic. Someone didn't like the fact that they had moved in there, and Billie was afraid that next time the person who had left the message would do something much worse.

It was as if everything had changed slightly after Simona's visit. Dad used to say that it was important to enjoy everyday life, because every-day life came along pretty often. And after three weeks in the house on Sparrisvägen, Billie realized that whether she liked it or not, Mum had created something like a normal, everyday life in their new home. Sometimes it was just the two of them, and sometimes they might have a visitor, but usually they did more or less the same things. Went to the beach, cooked, read, cleaned the house, did some gardening. They no longer talked about what had happened in the house, because if they did, Mum just got cross.

Almost against her will, Billie started to like her room with the sloping ceiling. She put up pictures of Dad and Grandma and Grandpa, and made space on the bookshelves for some of her own books which she had brought from town.

'I think you're going to be the first twelve-year-old in Sweden who has her very own library,' Mum said.

One rainy afternoon, Billie spent some time taking a closer look at her bookcase. She noticed that all the books were arranged in alphabetical order, according to the author's surname. Billie liked that, and added her own books in the same order. It looked good.

'Is your house still haunted?' Simona asked when she and Billie were chatting on the phone that evening.

'I don't think so,' Billie said. 'I haven't heard anything, anyway.'

That was why she hadn't made any further attempt to find Ella, the old lady who wanted to tell her terrible things about the house. Mum had got into the habit of locking the door of the spare room at bedtime, and Billie thought that was a good idea. She made sure she stayed upstairs during the night, and avoided going downstairs if Mum was asleep.

She saw Aladdin often – always in the village, or on the houseboat.

'Why don't you ask him round here?' Mum wanted to know.

Billie thought that was a stupid question. Aladdin was always alone on the boat, so of course it was much more fun to spend time there than at Billie's house.

But one afternoon Aladdin just turned up. Billie was sitting on the patio reading, and her mum had gone shopping. He looked really funny as he whizzed up the garden path on his unicycle.

'I thought it was time I saw your house,' he said. 'And I thought I might say hi to some of the ghosts.'

'I'd rather you didn't,' Billie replied.

'I see the paint's flaking off in places,' Aladdin said as he walked up the steps to the patio.

He pointed to one wall, where scraps of paint

had come loose and fallen to the ground. The cracks Billie had noticed on the very first day had multiplied and grown bigger, forming patterns on the walls.

'I know,' Billie said. 'Horrible, isn't it?'

It only took five minutes to show Aladdin around the house, and then they sat down on the patio with a glass of Mum's homemade blackcurrant juice.

'You found that comic in the spare room, didn't you?' Aladdin said.

'Mmm,' Billie said, staring into her glass.

'Weird,' Aladdin said.

It was a hot day, without a breath of wind or a cloud in the sky.

'Could I have some more juice?' Aladdin asked.

'Of course, I'll go and get some.'

Aladdin got up to go with Billie, but then he caught sight of the squirrel that sometimes played on the patio. Right now it was sitting on the lawn.

'Oh, how cute!' he said.

Billie was pleased. At last – something he didn't have down in the harbour! She went into the kitchen to fetch more juice while Aladdin stayed on the patio, watching the squirrel.

As she passed the doorway of the living room, she stopped. Something was bothering her, but she couldn't work out what it was. She stood there in silence, a glass of juice in each hand. Her mouth had gone completely dry. What was wrong?

Then she saw it.

The ceiling light was moving, just as it had done on the very first day when Billie was home alone.

Slowly it swung to and fro. As if someone was hanging from it.

Billie's heart started pounding again. How could the light be moving when the windows were closed, and there was no wind?

'Aladdin, can you come here?' she shouted,

turning towards the open door and the patio.

Aladdin must have heard from her voice that she was frightened, because a second later he was by her side. 'What's the matter?'

'Look,' Billie whispered, pointing to the antique ceiling light with one of the glasses she was holding.

The light wasn't moving at all.

'But . . .' Billie began. 'It was swinging to and fro just now!'

'Oh, I expect it was just a draught or something,' Aladdin said.

'A draught? There's no wind!' Billie said.

Then she heard Mum's voice from the garden.

'Not a word,' Billie said quickly to Aladdin.

Why did these things always happen to Billie, and not to Mum?

Aladdin looked confused, but promised to keep quiet.

Billie's mum was on her way up the steps with a carrier bag in each hand. Billie was still holding the glasses of juice, and Aladdin hurried forward to help Billie's mum.

'Oh, thank you!' she said. 'You must be Aladdin.'

It was the first time they had met, and Billie could see that her mum liked him. Then she saw something else. A tall man was walking up the steps behind Billie's mum. He smiled at Billie as if they knew one another.

'You must be Ebba's daughter,' he said.

Mum looked from the man to Billie. 'This is my friend Josef. I thought he could eat with us this evening.'

Chapter Eleven

It was a strange dinner. Aladdin stayed too. The man called Josef chatted and laughed, but Billie found it difficult to join in. Who was he, and what did he want?

Mum explained that Josef was a police officer who had helped her when someone tried to break into their house in town.

Billie stared at her. 'Someone tried to break in? Why didn't you say anything?'

Her mum looked away. 'I didn't want to worry you,' she said quietly. 'You've had some problems settling in here, and I didn't want to make things worse by telling you what had happened back in Kristianstad.'

'Why have you had problems settling in?' Josef asked. 'I think this is a lovely house.'

Billie didn't answer. She had no desire to talk about the house to someone she didn't know. Mum looked crossly at her.

'Well, for a start all the paint is peeling off,' Billie said eventually.

'Oh, that's nothing to worry about,' Josef said. 'That's the way things are with old houses. It's hard for them to find peace.'

To find peace. No, their house definitely hadn't found peace.

'Billie says she hears ghosts at night,' Mum said.

Josef laughed. 'Aren't you a bit old for that kind of thing?' he said.

Perhaps Billie should have thought before she acted, but she was so angry. She leaped to her feet and heard the chair crash to the ground behind her. 'You're just stupid!' she yelled at her mum. 'You're horrible! You don't think about anyone but yourself!'

She marched towards the house, turning round as she reached the doorway. 'What do you think Dad would have said if he could see you with a rotten copper?'

Once the words had left her mouth, it was too late. She couldn't take them back. Why on earth had she said such a thing? Mum looked terribly upset, and Josef dropped his fork.

Billie ran up to her room, thoroughly ashamed of herself. She had barely closed the door before it opened again. Aladdin walked in and shut the door behind him.

'Do you want to be on your own?'

Billie couldn't speak. If she opened her mouth, she would burst into tears. She sat down on the floor by the bookcase, and Aladdin sat down beside her.

'It was silly of your mum to joke about the ghosts,' he said.

Then the tears came. It was as if she was completely undone by the fact that someone was being nice to her.

'You don't believe me either,' she whispered.

Aladdin hesitated. 'To be honest, I don't really know what to think. As I told you, my mum believes in ghosts, but my dad and I don't.'

'I never said there were ghosts, I just said that weird, scary things keep happening in this house,' Billie said crossly, drying her eyes.

Aladdin looked at the bookcase. 'What lovely old books,' he said.

'They were here when we moved in.'

'What? You mean the previous owners didn't even take their books with them?'

The surprise in his voice made Billie feel all warm inside. It was so nice to find out that someone else felt the same way she did, and that she wasn't a crazy person who was just imagining things.

'They left behind a whole load of stuff,' she said.

She was about to tell him about the drawings she had moved from the desk when she spotted something that made her go cold.

Her own books were no longer in the bookcase. Someone had removed them and placed them in a pile on the floor. As if they weren't welcome among the other books. It couldn't possibly be Mum. She would never dream of touching Billie's beloved books.

Her finger shook as she pointed at the pile. 'I didn't put those there,' she whispered, suddenly afraid that there might be someone else in the room. 'Those are my books, and I put them on the shelves along with the old ones. In alphabetical order.'

Aladdin gazed at the books for a long time. 'So what do you want to do now?' he asked. 'Things can't go on like this.'

Billie drew her legs up to her chest and rested her chin on her knees. 'I just want everything to be all right again,' she said in a small voice.

'In that case, we'll sort it,' Aladdin said firmly.

'But how?'

'Good question. What is it that we want to know?'

Billie thought for a moment. 'We want to know who was tapping on my window that night. And who made the handprint on the table, then got out the comic and wrote *GO AWAY!* on it.'

Aladdin nodded as if he agreed. 'Anything else?'

Billie looked at the bookcase.

'Your books,' Aladdin said. 'Someone is obviously coming into the house without you or your mum realizing.'

'Exactly,' Billie said.

She could see that Aladdin was thinking something over.

'Do we think ghosts could be doing all this?'

On the one hand she didn't believe in ghosts and evil spirits. On the other hand ... She couldn't stop thinking about the ceiling light, swinging to and fro all by itself.

'I don't know,' she said. 'Maybe.'

'We need to try and find the family who used to live here,' Aladdin said. 'They have to tell us why they moved out so quickly. Bearing in mind all the things they left behind, you could almost believe they were fleeing for their lives.'

Billie shuddered. 'How are we going to find them?' she said. 'Shouldn't we speak to that old lady as well?'

Aladdin's dark eyes were shining. 'I've got an idea,' he said.

Chapter Twelve

'Where are you going?' Billie's mum said as Billie headed for the door with her cycle helmet looped over one arm and her rucksack on her back.

'Out. I'm meeting Aladdin.'

Her mum came out into the hallway with a tea towel in her hands. 'We need to talk about what happened yesterday, Billie. At dinner. When you walked out.'

Mum hadn't mentioned her outburst the previous evening, but had left her in peace.

Billie looked at the floor. 'Maybe we can talk later.'

Mum nodded, fiddling with the tea towel. 'Of course. I just want you to know that Josef is nothing more than a friend. A friend. Just as Aladdin is your friend. OK?'

The sadness came from nowhere, forming a solid lump in her throat. Mum gently stroked Billie's cheek.

'Say hello to Aladdin from me,' she said, and went back into the kitchen.

They met in the harbour by Aladdin's houseboat. Today he had got hold of a proper bike with two wheels.

'We'll start with the old lady from the library,' he said. 'She lives on Snickarhaksvägen, doesn't she?'

Billie wondered how Ella would react to Aladdin's presence, if they actually managed to find her. Hopefully she wouldn't insist on talking to Billie alone.

And she didn't. They cycled up and down

Snickarhaksvägen twice before Billie spotted her. She was sitting on the veranda of one of the smaller cottages, and was difficult to see from the road. When Billie and Aladdin turned onto her path, Ella practically flew up out of her chair.

'At last!' she cried.

Ella's cottage was full of candles, which she said she lit in the evenings. For some reason she insisted that they should talk indoors.

'Someone might see us if we sit on the veranda,' she said quietly.

Billie was very glad that Aladdin was there, because otherwise she wouldn't have been too happy about going into Ella's cottage and sitting there with the door shut.

The cottage was so small that it really consisted of only one room, housing a cooking area, a sofa, a bed and a small table.

Ella shuffled two cats off the sofa and invited Billie and Aladdin to sit down, while she sat on a wooden chair on the other side of the coffee table.

'How long have you been living in the house now?' she asked.

Billie and Aladdin looked at one another.

'It's only Billie who lives in the house,' Aladdin said. 'I live on a houseboat in the harbour.'

'I know exactly who you are,' Ella said. 'Your parents own the Turk in the Tower, don't they?'

Aladdin nodded, wide-eyed, and Billie saw Ella smile for the first time. She had lovely laughter lines around her eyes, and she actually looked really kind.

'We've lived in the house since the beginning of July,' she said.

She was surprised when she thought about it; was it really so long already? She would be back at school in only a week.

'How big is your family?' Ella wanted to know.

'There's only Mum and me.'

Ella sighed and shook her head. 'I'm glad it's just the two of you,' she said. 'But on the other hand, you've already lived in the house for too

90

long. You have to get out of there. The sooner the better!'

Ella's voice rose as she was speaking, and Billie remembered what the librarian had said – that Ella had a vivid imagination, and made things up to scare people.

'What's the rush?' Aladdin asked.

They were interrupted by the sound of rain on Ella's roof. Billie wasn't certain, but she thought she could hear the rumble of thunder far away in the distance. She hoped the storm would pass quickly, because she had no desire to be stuck in Ella's cottage for any longer than necessary.

Aladdin obviously felt the same, because he said impatiently: 'Can't you tell us what's so dangerous about the house?'

Ella leaned back in her chair. 'The youth of today,' she said wearily. 'You're so restless, you never have time to stop and think about things properly.'

One of the cats that she had chased off the

sofa jumped up on her lap. Ella stroked its back. After a while she looked at Billie and said: 'I have to confess right from the start that I don't know everything. But I do know some things, enough to be sure that the house you live in is not normal.'

At that point there was a clap of thunder so loud that both Billie and Aladdin jumped.

Ella looked out of the window. 'It's over fifty years since I visited your house for the first time,' she said. 'And I realized right away that something was terribly wrong.'

Chapter Thirteen

Once upon a time, Ella had worked as a cleaner for various families in Åhus, and some of those families had lived in Billie's house.

'It was the end of the 1950s,' Ella said. 'I was supposed to clean the house twice a week. The children who lived there were pale and frightened. At first I assumed they were afraid of their father. He was a big, noisy fellow who shouted at his family, and no doubt beat them as well.'

She broke off when she saw the horrified expression on Billie and Aladdin's faces.

'Things were different back then,' she said. 'In those days people were allowed to smack their children. I didn't like going there – what if he decided to start on me as well?'

Aladdin squirmed on the sofa. He was still impatient, but waited politely for Ella to continue.

'I soon realized that it wasn't the father that was the family's problem. No, it was the house itself. They weren't alone there, you see.'

She fixed her big eyes on Billie. 'You know what I'm talking about, don't you?'

In spite of the fact that she wasn't at all sure, Billie nodded. 'I think so.'

At the sound of the next thunderclap, the cats ran and hid under the table.

'They're such cowards,' Ella muttered.

Billie would have liked to hide under a table as well, but instead she edged closer to Aladdin on the sofa.

'Have you seen the ceiling light in the living room moving?' Ella asked.

Billie could feel her cheeks flush red. So she hadn't been imagining things after all!

'Oh yes,' Ella went on. 'It doesn't matter what kind of light you put up in there, it will always swing to and fro.'

'Not all the time,' Billie said.

'No, but at some point every day.'

'Why does it do that?' Aladdin asked.

Suddenly Ella looked unsure of herself. 'I don't really know how much I ought to tell you,' she said. 'You're only children, after all.'

'I think we can cope,' Aladdin said, straightening up. 'Can't we, Billie?'

'Of course,' Billie said, but her voice came out as no more than a whisper.

'In that case,' Ella said resolutely, 'they say that the light in that room moves because a young woman died there. I don't know who she was or why she did it, but according to what I've heard, a very unhappy girl lived in the house at one time. And she hanged herself from the hook on the ceiling in the living room.'

This was worse than anything Billie had imagined Ella might say.

'Did she die?' she said. 'The girl who hanged herself?'

'Of course she did,' Aladdin said.

'And now she's haunting us because we live in the house?'

Ella pursed her lips. 'I'm not sure about haunting – it sounds a bit childish when you put it like that. I'd prefer to say that the house is cursed.'

Billie and Aladdin looked at one another. Cursed?

'What does that mean?' Billie said.

'That things go badly for anyone who lives there. I worked as a cleaner for four different families in that house. None of them stayed for longer than three years. Something terrible happened to all of them. I have no idea how many families have lived there since then, but it shouldn't be difficult to find out.'

'What kind of things happened to them?' Aladdin wondered.

'All sorts,' Ella said. 'In the first family – you remember, the one with the horrible father – the eldest son fell down the stairs and broke his leg in three places. And he hit his head as well. In the next family the mother was hurt. The kitchen stove caught fire and burned her face.'

'Yes, but accidents happen all the time,' Aladdin said sceptically. 'People fall down the stairs and old stoves catch fire – that doesn't just happen in Billie's house.'

'You don't think it seems strange that so many accidents have happened in that particular house?' Ella said.

'Maybe, maybe not,' Aladdin replied.

'Bad things have happened in that house ever since it was built,' Ella said firmly. 'If I remember rightly, it was a school to begin with. I know that there was a lot of gossip about it when I first came here. There was talk of a school that had to be closed because there were problems with the children who went there. People talked about the glass children.'

Billie and Aladdin looked at one another again.

'The glass children?' Billie said.

'Apparently that was what they called the children who attended the school in your house, but I have no idea why.'

Nor had Billie, but she really wanted to find out.

'Do you know why the previous family moved out?' Ella said, looking straight at Billie.

'No,' Billie said. 'Do you?'

'No, but I think you ought to look into it. Because they certainly didn't stay there for very long.'

'They were in such a hurry to leave that they didn't even take their furniture,' Billie said.

Ella looked surprised. 'What furniture?'

'More or less everything, I think. They just left. The whole house was full of stuff when they moved out last summer.'

'Goodness me,' Ella whispered, getting to her feet.

Without another word she went over to the sink and poured herself a glass of water. She didn't ask whether Billie and Aladdin might be thirsty too.

'Who told you they moved out last summer?' she said.

'The man who showed us around the house,' Billie said. 'His name was Martin.'

Ella had another drink. 'I don't know who that man is,' she said slowly. 'But I do know that no one has lived in that house on a permanent basis for the last two years. And as far as the furniture is concerned . . .' She paused. 'Have you seen a little metal table covered in small, brightly coloured tiles?'

The table on which Billie had found the hand-print.

'It's in our spare room,' she said quietly.

'Oh my goodness,' Ella whispered.

She put down the glass and leaned against the draining board, supporting herself with one hand as if she was afraid she might fall over.

'That table was there when I first went to the house more than fifty years ago,' she said. 'The house was always sold as a furnished property in the past. Don't ask me why, but that's the way it was. All the families I worked for had more or less the same furniture. And now here you are fifty years later, telling me that it's all still there.'

Billie got up, and Aladdin did the same. What Ella said couldn't possibly be true. Why would the man who showed them the house have lied about both the furniture and when the previous owners moved out? To be fair, he had lied about other things as well, but nothing as serious. Or had he?

'We have to go,' Billie said. 'But thank you for letting us come to see you.'

'You're welcome to come again if you have any more questions,' Ella said.

The rain was still hammering in the roof, and the sky was lit up over and over again by vivid flashes of lightning. They would be soaked to the skin before they got back to their side of the harbour.

But Billie wasn't thinking about the storm. She was thinking about the ceiling light in the living room, and the glass children. Could it really be true that someone had died in their house? And who were the glass children?

Chapter Fourteen

Even though she had a feeling it was a bad idea, Billie couldn't help telling her mum what she had found out when she got home.

At first her mum didn't say anything.

'Couldn't you have a word with our neighbours?' Billie said to fill the silence.

'About what?'

'About when they last saw people living here. If the house has been empty for several years, they must have noticed.'

Billie had been so wound up when they left Ella that she had cycled all the way back to

Sparrisvägen instead of going to the houseboat with Aladdin.

And now she was standing in the hallway, bubbling over with everything she had heard. She was soaking wet, dripping all over the floor.

'Billie,' her mum said seriously. 'Is it Aladdin who's come up with this idea that the house is haunted?'

Aladdin? What was she talking about? Things had been happening in the house before Billie even met him.

'No,' she said. 'And I never said it was haunted, just that—'

'You know what,' her mum broke in. 'I will actually speak to the neighbours as soon as I have time. Because we have to get to the bottom of all this.'

Billie was pleased.

Her mum said softly, 'How about this: I'll speak to the neighbours. And if they say that the family moved out last summer, and not two years

103

ago as that old gossip claims, then you stop all this nonsense about there being something wrong with this house. OK?'

Billie thought for a moment. They hardly knew the neighbours; they could say anything at all. But she didn't dare challenge her mum on that particular point, or she wouldn't speak to them at all.

'OK,' she said reluctantly.

Her mum was relieved. 'Good! Now hop in the shower and get yourself warm before dinner.'

At that moment the phone rang, and her mum rushed to answer.

'Josef – how are you?' Billie heard her say.

Slowly she went into the bathroom and started to pull off her wet clothes. She suddenly felt very lonely.

That night Billie couldn't sleep. She tried every trick in the book, but it was no good. Eventually she gave up and switched on the reading lamp that her mum had put up above the bed.

Billie glanced at the clock and sighed. It was almost midnight. She picked up the book that was lying on her bedside table. She would read a chapter or two before she made another attempt to get to sleep.

But although her eyes read one word after another, Billie's thoughts were elsewhere. Everything Ella had told her was flying around inside her head like lost butterflies.

Aladdin had been sceptical when they left the old lady's cottage. 'Did she tell us one single thing that was of any use to us?' he had said.

Billie had felt obliged to stick up for Ella. 'She said that bad things had happened to several families who lived in our house, just as you'd heard in school. And remember what she said about the light in the living room. I've actually seen it moving.'

'We need to find out if the rest is true,' Aladdin had said. 'What she said about the house having been empty for two years rather than one.'

'And don't forget what she said about the furniture,' Billie had added. 'And the children who were known as the glass children.'

When she got home she had sat down at the computer and tried to find information about both their house and the glass children. She hadn't come up with a thing.

Billie had decided that this didn't make any difference. Ella could still be right. The very idea that the furniture in the house could be more than fifty years old, and hadn't actually belonged to the previous family, made Billie feel scared. In that case there was definitely something wrong.

Billie had just switched off her reading lamp when she heard it. Just like when Simona had stayed over.

Something was tapping on the window.

Tap, tap.

Oh no.

Billie curled up under the covers.

Not now. Not when she was all on her own.

The distance to her mum's room suddenly seemed endless, as if her mum was on a different planet. There was no chance that Billie would be brave enough to get out of bed while someone was tapping on the window.

She held her breath and waited and waited. At long last the tapping stopped, but still she didn't dare move. Not until after a considerable amount of time had passed did she lift her head off the pillow. She listened as hard as she could, sitting in the darkness for ages with a pounding heart as she waited for the sound to come back.

But nothing happened. After a while she kicked off the covers and got out of bed. She didn't have the nerve to look out of the window as Simona had done, but stood there in the middle of the floor listening, until she was absolutely certain that everything was quiet. Only then was she able to breathe out.

Slowly Billie's heartbeat returned to normal. She briefly considered calling Aladdin or Simona, but realized that they were probably asleep. It would be best if she went back to bed too.

But she needed the loo.

She wouldn't be able to sleep until she had been for a wee. Oh no!

Billie's whole body was on full alert as she crept out of her room. She didn't switch on the light because she didn't want to wake her mum. She ran silently down the stairs and into the bathroom. She closed and locked the door, and did what she had to do as quickly as possible.

When she came out into the hallway, she noticed that the door of the spare room was open. The door that Mum always locked at bedtime, ever since Billie and Simona had gone in there during the night.

Billie swallowed hard. Perhaps Mum had just forgotten to lock the door tonight.

Or perhaps . . .

She couldn't just go back to bed – she had to know. Her body was as taut as a violin string as she covered the short distance to the spare room and looked inside.

Everything was as it should be.

Or was it? There was something on the little table where Billie and Simona had found the comic. But this time it wasn't a comic.

Billie was drawn towards the table as if it was a magnet. Someone had laid out one of the drawings that she had put away on the very first day. But that wasn't all.

On top of the drawing someone had placed two small figures, two little glass statues representing a boy and a girl. Both children had serious faces, and were dressed in old-fashioned clothes. The colours painted on the glass had faded, but you could still see that the girl was wearing a red dress and the boy a blue shirt.

Glass children, Billie thought. Just like the ones Ella had talked about.

Then she saw what someone had written on the drawing:

Stop looking. Otherwise this will end badly.

Chapter Fifteen

It was Aladdin who worked out how to discover the name of the family who used to live in Billie's house.

'There must be a contract,' he said. 'When your mum bought the house, she must have signed a document with the name of the other family on it.'

Of course, Billie thought.

She had stopped talking to her mum about all the strange goings-on in the house; there was just no point. As a result she was talking to Aladdin even more, and he too was afraid when she showed him the drawing she had found in the spare room, and told him about the glass children on the table.

'I was so scared I didn't get a wink of sleep all night,' Billie said miserably.

'*Stop looking*,' Aladdin read. 'This house certainly holds onto its secrets.'

Billie nodded. But she had no intention of allowing herself to be frightened. If the house had secrets, then she wanted to know what they were. Tracking down the previous family seemed like a good start, which meant they had to find out their name.

The next time her mum went off to the shops, Billie seized the opportunity. She ran into Mum's room to look for the contract. Her mum wasn't particularly good at keeping things in order. In fact, she was hopeless. Dad had been responsible for all that, making sure bills and documents ended up in the right folders.

Billie knew that her mum kept 'important

stuff' in one of her desk drawers. She had shown it to Billie once; there was a spare front door key, their passports, and a few other things that might be useful. Billie guessed that the contract would be considered important.

Mum's room was exactly the same shape as Billie's, with a sloping ceiling and a window set in the gable. But the furniture was different, and so were the colours. Just like Billie, Mum had kept all the furniture except the bed, and it was obvious that this had been an adult's room. All the furniture was made of wood, and it was all brown. Even the armchair in one corner was brown.

Could the furniture really be as old as Ella had said? Billie tried out the armchair and felt herself sink into the stuffing. Next to the chair stood a spinning wheel and a little stool. Billie closed her eyes, picturing someone sitting on the stool and spinning away. Quickly she opened her eyes. She didn't like being in the house all on her own, and she didn't want to spend any more time thinking about how old the furniture was.

The most important thing was the contract.

Billie's hand was shaking as she tried the drawer. It wasn't locked, but it was quite stiff.

Mum would be away for at least an hour, which was just as well, because the contents of the drawer were a complete mess. Billie didn't want her mum to know that she had been rummaging around, so she lifted the papers carefully to see if she could find what she was looking for. She saw bills and receipts and pay slips, but no contract.

The sound of birds on the roof made her stiffen. Sometimes they were there, sometimes they weren't. It was the same at night. Sometimes the birds didn't make a sound, but sometimes they made so much noise that they woke her up.

Billie was just about to give up and start searching for the contract in Mum's messy bookcase instead when she spotted an open envelope in the drawer. She took it out and squeezed it. It seemed to contain a thick wad of papers. Billie could feel her excitement growing as she pulled everything out and read the top sheet. *Contract of Sale*, it said.

At last! She glanced at the page and found both her mum's name and their address in town. Further down she discovered what she was looking for:

Vendors: David and Marie Stjärnguld

Billie felt a flush of pleasure. David and Marie Stjärnguld, that was their name. She thought it was rather an odd surname, but it was also good to have such an unusual name. A bit like Aladdin – that was different too, but in a good way. She carried on reading, and was disappointed to learn that if she had understood the contract correctly, the family had moved to Germany.

Billie's heart sank. Germany was a long way

from Åhus. She looked through the contract carefully – perhaps they had left a telephone number or an address where they could be reached? But there was nothing.

She tucked the contract back in the envelope and replaced it in the drawer. She would go and see Aladdin right away. They mustn't give up too easily. The family lived too far away to visit, and there was no way they could phone them either. But at least they had a name now.

There couldn't be many people called Stjärnguld.

Chapter Sixteen

Aladdin gazed at Billie's notebook where she had written down the name of the family.

'What do we do now?' Billie said. 'How are we going to find out why they moved? Should we cycle round the village and ask if anyone knew the Stjärnguld family when they lived here?'

They were sitting in Aladdin's room. The harbour was still busy with people looking at the boats and eating ice cream, but Billie thought you could tell that the summer was coming to an end. She couldn't wait to get back to school – she would be in Kristianstad every day.

Aladdin went and fetched a laptop and tried a few searches. The Stjärnguld family was nowhere to be found. Without saying a word he put down the computer and started looking for something on the shelf above his bed. After a while he found what he was after.

'I knew I'd kept them,' he said, pulling out several books.

He sat down next to Billie. 'Yearbooks,' he said.

Billie looked. One for every year Aladdin had been in school. There weren't many schools in Åhus, and they all shared a yearbook. There were class photos of everyone who had attended primary, junior or high school in Åhus over the past few years.

Aladdin passed her two of the yearbooks. 'How many people do you think are called Stjärnguld? If we find any kids by that name in here, then I'm certain they must belong to the family who used to live in your house.'

It didn't take long to flick through the yearbooks. Billie looked at the photographs, and was very pleased that she would be staying on at her old school in town. She didn't recognize a single person.

The first book she looked at was from the school year before last, the one that had finished last summer. That was when the family had moved out, according to the old man who had shown Billie and her mum around the house. If that was true, and if the family had children, then they should be in this yearbook.

But they weren't.

'Maybe they were off sick on the day the photographer came in,' Aladdin said.

'That doesn't make any difference,' Billie said. 'Look, there's a list of everyone who was absent that day.'

She looked through the book from last year. There was no one in high school called Stjärnguld. Nor in the junior or primary schools.

What if the children had gone to school in Kristianstad, just like Billie? She had better look through her own yearbooks as well when she got home.

The boat suddenly swayed, and Billie glanced up.

'Have you finished?' Aladdin asked. 'I didn't find anything.'

That was when Billie saw the girl's name. It was under the very last picture in the yearbook, which showed fifteen children in the first year.

Wilma Stjärnguld.

She was sitting right on the end of the bottom row. Her hair was like Simona's, thick and curly, although she was blonde rather than ginger.

Billie and Aladdin gazed at the picture for a long time. Wilma Stjärnguld had started in the first year three years ago, but she wasn't in any of the later yearbooks. So Ella might have been right when she said that the family had moved two years ago, not last year.

What else had the man who showed them the house lied about?

'We'll go over to her school,' Aladdin said. 'We might find something out if we speak to the teachers.'

'But there won't be anyone there,' Billie said. 'Don't the teachers have a summer holiday like us?'

'They go back two weeks before us,' Aladdin said. 'To plan our lessons and sort out the timetable.'

Aladdin led the way as they set off on their bikes. He hadn't gone to this particular school, but some of his friends had.

The school was silent and deserted. Billie counted the buildings; there were three small red-painted blocks, plus a slightly bigger one that she assumed was the gym.

'Let's find the staffroom,' Aladdin said, tugging at her arm.

They walked round the buildings and peered in through the windows. In the block furthest away they could see a number of adults coming and going in the various rooms.

'This must be it,' Billie said, just as a man with a cup of coffee in his hand caught sight of her.

Instinctively Billie crouched down so that she disappeared from view.

'What are you doing?' Aladdin said. 'We want them to see us and come to the door, don't we?'

Billie felt stupid.

A second later the door opened and the man with the coffee cup came out onto the steps.

'Is there something I can help you with?' he said.

Chapter Seventeen

Billie thought the man looked really nice. He was wearing a comfy old green jumper and baggy jeans.

'We were wondering if you know a girl called Wilma Stjärnguld,' Aladdin said. 'Or if any of the other teachers might know her.'

The man frowned. 'Why do you ask?'

'We want to find out if she's a pupil here,' Aladdin said, even though they knew perfectly well that she wasn't. 'Billie here has moved into the Stjärnguld family's house. May we come in?'

When Aladdin said where Billie lived, the man

almost dropped his coffee cup. 'Of course, come on in,' he said, taking a step back.

Billie and Aladdin followed him inside.

'I'm not sure I understand what it is that you want to know,' the man said. 'But I was Wilma's class teacher.'

'Oh,' Billie said; she was getting to be almost as good a liar as Aladdin. 'So she doesn't live in Åhus any more?'

'No, the family moved away two years ago.'

Billie hardly dared breathe. So Ella had been right.

'Do you know where they went?' Aladdin asked.

'Abroad, I think,' the man said, taking a sip of his coffee.

'Why did they move?' Billie said.

The man looked at her for a long time, then glanced at his watch. 'I have no idea,' he said. 'I'm afraid I really don't have time to stand here chatting.'

He sounded cross. Or afraid?

'Is there anyone else who might know more?' Aladdin said.

'No, there isn't,' the teacher replied. 'Now off you go.'

'He was a bit weird,' Aladdin said when they were back in the playground.

Billie agreed. 'I think he was lying,' she said. 'And I think he knew more than he was willing to tell us.'

'I think you're right,' Aladdin said.

Billie searched her pockets for the key to her bicycle lock. 'Let's go back to yours,' she said. 'I need the loo.'

'Can't you go here instead?' Aladdin said. 'I thought we could go for an ice cream.'

Billie glanced over towards the school.

'Come on,' Aladdin said. 'All you have to do is go in and find the toilets.'

I'm such a coward most of the time, Billie thought. *Simona wouldn't have hesitated for a second.*

'Wait here, I'll be as quick as I can,' she said firmly, running back towards the block they had just left.

This time she didn't wait for someone to come and open the door, but slipped inside. She hurried along the corridor looking for a toilet. She sincerely hoped no one would spot her.

A door on the right was standing open, and she could hear voices from inside the room.

She recognized one of the voices; it was the man with the coffee cup.

'I didn't know what to say,' he said.

A woman answered: 'You did the right thing. Children shouldn't have to hear what happened.'

Billie stood perfectly still, listening hard.

'She was always so frightened of everything,' the man said with a sigh. 'The child looked as if she could see ghosts in broad daylight.'

'Wilma was different,' the woman said. 'Just like that house.'

'The girl who was here asking about Wilma claims that she lives in the house now.'

Billie heard the woman gasp.

'That can't be true,' she said. 'It seems completely impossible to have a good life at that address.'

'Yes, but none of us believes in ghouls and ghosts,' the man said. 'All those stories about the house on Sparrisvägen ... Can they really be true?'

'I think they ought to tear that house down and build a new one,' the woman muttered. 'It's obviously going to get harder and harder to find new owners. I mean, it's been empty for quite some time now.'

'Let's hope it all works out better for the family who are living there now,' the man said quietly. 'It would be terrible if more people came to grief.'

'Absolutely,' said the woman. 'It started with the glass children, and things haven't been right since. Poor Wilma. Do you remember what she told us? She couldn't sleep because someone kept tapping on her window. And she said that someone went into her room when no one was home and moved her toys around.'

'You can understand why her parents didn't believe her,' the man said. 'Although of course everything changed when she almost drowned. They certainly moved fast then.'

'And not a day too soon,' the woman said. 'After all, someone had tried to drag her under the water.'

Billie didn't know what to do with herself. So someone had tried to drown Wilma! That was why the family had moved out so suddenly.

With her heart pounding, Billie ran back to Aladdin. No one was safe in the house on Sparrisvägen, that much was clear.

Chapter Eighteen

Mum's holiday came to an end, and Billie was poorly. She had a temperature and a sore throat, and had to stay in bed.

'Have you got enough books?' her mum said anxiously before she left for work.

'Yes,' Billie said, thinking that the problem with spending a whole day home alone was unlikely to be a lack of reading material, but that the house she lived in was extremely dangerous.

Her mum sighed, looking worried. 'I don't like the idea of leaving you on your own when you're not well,' she said.

'I'll be fine,' Billie said.

'There's food in the fridge for you to heat up.'

Mum bent down and kissed her on the forehead. 'I'll call you later,' she said. 'You take care of yourself. Promise.'

Billie promised.

Then she remembered that she'd forgotten to ask her mum about something. 'Have you spoken to the neighbours yet?' she said.

Billie hadn't told her mum what she and Aladdin had learned about the family they had bought the house from, but she was curious about what her mum might have found out from the neighbours.

Her mum looked surprised. 'The neighbours? No – what do you mean?'

'You said you'd ask them about the family who used to live here, find out when they moved out.'

Her mum didn't speak for a moment. 'That's right,' she said. 'Yes, I did speak to them.'

Billie sat bolt upright in bed. In that case Mum

must know that they had moved out two years ago, not last year! 'What did they say?' she asked eagerly.

Her mum scratched her forehead and screwed up her eyes as if she was thinking about something really complicated. 'They said they moved out a year ago, just as Martin told us when he showed us the house.'

'But . . .' Billie didn't know what to say. Someone was lying – either Mum or the neighbours. Billie guessed it was Mum.

Her mum looked at her watch. 'I have to go,' she said. 'You remember what you promised me, don't you?'

Billie lay back down. What had she promised?

'You said that if I spoke to the neighbours, you would stop all this nonsense about there being something wrong with this house. Do you remember?'

'Yes.'

There was no point in talking to Mum any

more. They would only end up falling out.

Mum looked relieved. 'Excellent. That's the end of that, then. Now you look after yourself, sweetheart. I'll be home as early as I can this afternoon.'

Her footsteps made the stairs creak, then Billie heard the front door close. Mum had lied to her.

Perhaps it was because she had a temperature and was sleeping a lot, but after a while Billie started to think that it was rather nice to be home alone. The sun came and went, but it wasn't too hot, and Billie left the window open. Their neighbour seemed to be cutting the grass, and Billie liked to hear that sound. When Dad was alive, he had been very particular about keeping the lawn nice.

'It's the first thing people see when they look at the house,' he used to say.

He would be out there working hard to achieve the perfect lawn while Billie and her mum stood at the kitchen window, giggling away. It was a long time since they had laughed like that.

Just after lunch there was a knock on the door. Billie froze in her bed. People hardly ever called round. She tiptoed down the stairs and said, 'Who's there?' before she unlocked the door.

'It's only me!'

Aladdin, of course.

'I'm not very well,' Billie said as she let him in.

'I know that. I thought you might be fed up, so I've come to see you. Can I stay for a while?'

Billie smiled. 'Of course you can.'

They went and sat on the patio, with Aladdin swinging in the hammock and Billie a little distance away.

'How long will you stay on the houseboat?' Billie asked.

'Until I go back to school next week.'

They sat in silence for a few moments.

'Has anything happened over the past few

days?' Aladdin asked. 'In the house, I mean.'

Billie shook her head. No, everything had been quiet.

Then she told him that her mum had lied.

'She doesn't believe you,' Aladdin said. 'That's why she did it.'

'I know,' Billie said. 'I think we're running out of time. We have to find out more about the house so that I can make her understand how dangerous it is.'

She thought about what the teacher had said about Wilma Stjärnguld: that she had heard tapping on the windows, and no one had believed her.

'If it's only children who see all these terrible things, I'll never be able to convince Mum,' Billie said.

Aladdin didn't reply; he was staring at something behind her back. 'Look,' he whispered.

Billie turned round. She could see through the hallway and into the living room. Aladdin was pointing at the ceiling light. It was swinging silently to and fro, just as Billie had seen it do before.

Even though it was the middle of the day, Billie was every bit as frightened as she had been at night. The sun had disappeared behind the clouds, and she shivered.

She no longer had any doubts. The house was haunted. And the ghost wouldn't leave them alone until they moved out.

Chapter Nineteen

More and more paint started flaking off the out-side of the house. More and more scraps of blue littered the ground, and yellow patches began to appear all over the walls.

'I just don't understand it,' her mum said as she and Billie took a walk around the house to look at the patches.

Billie was better, and the summer holidays were over. She was glad that term had started. Everything was more enjoyable now that she knew she only had to spend the evenings and nights in the house. Although of course the evenings and nights were the worst.

Mum called Josef to ask him to come and look at the outside walls. Billie thought the house was shaking off the blue paint, because it didn't like the fact that it had been repainted. It was doing the same thing with the paint as it had done with everyone who had tried to live in the house – it simply got rid of them.

Aladdin and his parents left the houseboat and moved back into their house. Aladdin had to go to school in Åhus as usual, and he and Billie didn't see each other as often. But they called each other every evening.

'We have to find out more about the house,' Aladdin said. 'We can't stop now, not until we've managed to persuade your mum that it's dangerous.'

Their house in town hadn't yet been sold, and Billie was hoping that they would be able to expose the secret of the house in Åhus before someone bought it. Then they could simply move back home. Aladdin looked sad when she said that.

'I'd come and visit you,' Billie said. 'Often!'

But it wouldn't be the same, and she knew it. If she moved away from Åhus she would lose Aladdin, and if she stayed she would drift away from her friends in town. She noticed that Simona behaved differently towards her when they went back to school.

'Would you like to come home with me one day after school?' Billie asked. 'Mum says you can stay over.'

Simona snorted. 'Oh, so you've got time for me after all, have you? I thought you were only hanging out with Aladdin these days.'

Billie was hurt. 'That's not fair,' she said. 'It's just that so much has happened over the summer. And you've been away for several weeks!'

Eventually Simona stopped sulking, and at the end of the first week she went home with Billie on the Friday afternoon.

'What's happened to the paint?' she said in astonishment as they cycled up the path and she saw the house.

'I'll tell you all about it!' Billie promised.

They sat on the patio having a snack, while Billie talked and talked about everything that had gone on. She explained what she and Aladdin had done after Simona went home.

'Oh, I wish I'd been here!' Simona said. 'It must have been so exciting!'

But Billie didn't really agree. She thought it had all been terrible, rather than exciting.

'So what's your next move?' Simona asked, taking a bite of her cinnamon bun.

'We thought we might go to the library in Kristianstad to ask if they know where you can get information on old houses.'

That had been Aladdin's idea.

'The library?' Simona said. 'Couldn't you find anything on the internet?'

'We've searched and searched, but we didn't

come up with a thing,' Billie said. 'I think this is all too far in the past to be on the net.'

'If you're going to the library, then I want to come too,' Simona said firmly.

She didn't want to be left out again, and Billie said she was welcome to join them. Simona's friendship was important to her, and she didn't want to fall out. She had enough problems already.

And there were more to come. It all began when Simona had gone home on Saturday. Mum had a headache and went to lie down in the middle of the day. Billie was left alone with Josef, who had come to look at the paint.

'You have to take care of old houses,' he said. 'And I don't think the previous owners did that. Look at this.'

He showed Billie. 'You can't just repaint a house over and over again. Sooner or later you have to strip off all the old paint, and start again from the beginning.'

Start again from the beginning. That was exactly what the house didn't want.

'You ought to get back some of the money you paid for this place,' Josef said. 'The previous owners should have told you about the paint.'

Billie was delighted. She hoped the problem would be so big that Mum would want all her money back, not just some of it. Then they could move back home again.

Aladdin came round and they played games with Josef. Mum wasn't well enough to join in, and stayed in bed.

'What's the matter with her?' Aladdin asked.

'She's got a headache,' Billie said.

Josef looked anxious. 'I think it's more than that, Billie,' he said. 'She's starting to get a temperature, just like you had.'

Billie couldn't help worrying when Mum was ill. She had felt that way ever since Dad died.

Josef made something to eat, but Mum wasn't

interested. At ten o'clock Aladdin had to go home.

'I'll call you tomorrow,' he said.

Billie was about to go to bed when Josef said: 'I can stay if you like. If you're worried about your mum.'

She hesitated. Where would he sleep? The spare room was still full of stuff.

'I can sleep on the sofa,' he said when he realized why she hadn't answered.

Billie really wanted him to go home, but she had a strong feeling that she would regret it if she turned down his offer.

'I'll go and find you some bedding,' she said.

It was almost midnight, and Billie was still reading in bed. She was wide awake. Every time she tried to put down her book, her mind started spinning. She thought back to what someone had written on the drawing she had found in the spare room.

142

Stop looking.

But she had carried on digging into events and people from long ago. What if something terrible happened because of what she had done?

Eventually she must have fallen asleep, because when she woke up it was still dark, but the house was full of noise. Someone was whimpering, and a man's voice said: 'Be careful, the stairs are pretty narrow!'

Billie flew out of bed and ran onto the landing. Two men were carrying something down the stairs. It took a moment for Billie to realize that it was a stretcher, and that her mum was lying on it.

Josef caught Billie and wrapped his arms around her when she tried to run after the stretcher.

'Let go of me!' she screamed.

'Everything is all right,' Josef said, but she could hear that he was afraid. 'It's just that your mum was in so much pain with her headache that I had to call an ambulance. I couldn't drive her to the hospital myself and leave you here on your own. Your mum didn't want me to do that either.'

Billie started to cry.

The ghost had got what it wanted. Mum was ill, and had to go to hospital in an ambulance. What if she didn't get better?

Who would look after Billie then?

Chapter Twenty

'Meningitis,' the doctor said to Billie and Josef.

Billie was so scared that she slipped her hand into Josef's. He squeezed it hard.

'But she will get better, won't she?' she said.

'I'm sure she will,' the doctor replied. 'But it's going to take some time. It's just as well that you came in as quickly as you did. If you'd waited until morning, things would have been much more serious.'

'How long will she have to stay in hospital?' Josef asked.

'Hard to say. We'll wait a few days and see how she's feeling then.'

The doctor looked at his papers and asked: 'Has she been ill much lately?'

Both Billie and Josef shook their heads.

The doctor shrugged. 'In that case it's just sheer bad luck,' he said. 'It's unfortunate, but these things happen.'

Billie wanted to open her mouth and yell that it definitely wasn't sheer bad luck that her mum had been taken ill. She was ill because they lived in a dreadful house. But enough was enough. As soon as Billie got home, she would call Aladdin and Simona. She and her mum had to get away from that house before something even worse happened; there was no time to lose.

'Shall we call someone, or will you be taking care of the child?' the doctor asked Josef, glancing at Billie. 'As I understand it you're just a friend of the family.'

'We'll sort it out,' Josef said. 'There's no need to call anyone.'

Josef and Billie had already discussed the matter in the car on their way to the hospital. They had decided to get in touch with Grandma and Grandpa to see if they could come over and look after Billie.

They were allowed to sit with Billie's mum for a little while, then they drove back to Åhus.

'We need to get some sleep,' Josef said.

Only then did Billie realize how tired she was. When she felt the cool sheets against her skin, she relaxed and closed her eyes. The last thing she heard before she fell asleep was the birds, scampering about on the roof.

Grandma was ill too, so she and Grandpa couldn't come and look after Billie.

'It's nothing serious,' Grandma said. 'It's just an ordinary cold, and I've got a bit of a temperature. But it's probably best if we don't come into contact with you and your mum at the moment; what if I were to pass something on to her, and she got even worse?'

Billie agreed, so they arranged for Josef to move in and sleep on the sofa while Mum was in hospital. Aladdin came rushing over with a message from his parents to say that Billie was very welcome to stay with them instead, but she preferred to stay at home. Josef gave her a lift to school in the mornings, and in the afternoons she went to the hospital to see her mum. Josef picked her up from there when he finished work.

Aladdin came round to see Billie every evening.

'We have to go to the library,' he said when Billie's mum had been in hospital for three days. 'We can't wait any longer.'

'We'll go tomorrow,' Billie said firmly.

'We need to find out why the paint is peeling off,' Josef said over dinner. 'Or, to put it more accurately – why it *was* peeling off. It seems to have stopped now. We'll get someone who knows about these things to take a look at it.'

Billie didn't say anything. First the paint was falling off, and then it wasn't. She hadn't heard any tapping or other noises at night, and there had been no more messages in the spare room, even though she had gone and looked two nights in a row. It was as if the house was holding its breath, waiting for what was going to happen next.

'How are you getting on with Josef?' Mum asked when Billie spoke to her on the phone that evening. She sounded tired and anxious.

'Fine,' Billie said. 'But I still want you to hurry up and get better.'

'I'm doing my best, sweetheart,' Mum said.

That was probably true, because the doctor said that Mum was improving and would be allowed home soon. He had told Billie several times how badly things could have gone if her mum hadn't been brought into hospital.

Billie tried to imagine what her life would have been like if she had lost Mum too, but it was just too painful to think about. If Mum died, Billie would be the loneliest person in the world.

Chapter Twenty-One

The library in Kristianstad was square, with big blocks of stone on the walls.

Billie and Simona met Aladdin off the bus from Åhus and walked to the library. It was much bigger than the one in Åhus, but Billie didn't think it was anywhere near as appealing.

'There's someone we can ask,' Aladdin said, pointing to a young man who was sitting there sorting books.

There was a sign above his desk that said INFORMATION. He looked pleased to see them. 'Please sit down,' he said, gesturing towards three chairs in front of his desk. 'How can I help you?'

'I'd like to find out more about the house I live in,' Billie said.

Aladdin and Simona were just as keen as Billie.

'It must be possible,' Aladdin said.

'I'm sure it is,' said the young man. 'Is there something special about the house? I mean, is it famous? Is it a palace?'

Billie looked at her friends. She wasn't sure whether famous was the right word. Everyone in Åhus seemed to know about it, but before Billie moved there, she'd never heard of it. And it definitely wasn't a palace.

'Strange things keep happening in the house,' Aladdin said. 'That's why we want to know more.'

Billie hesitated, but eventually she said: 'We think it might be haunted.'

She blushed as she spoke. Surely nobody of her age actually believed in ghosts these days!

'I understand,' said the young man. 'What's the address?'

Billie told him, and he thought for a moment.

'Come with me,' he said, getting to his feet.

He led them to one of the bookshelves right at the back of the library.

'This is where we keep books on what we call spirits, which is roughly the same as ghosts. Perhaps you could start by having a look through this one?'

He took down a thick volume and handed it to Billie. She read the title: *Haunted Houses from North to South*.

'That means that spirits and ghosts won't leave these houses in peace,' the young man explained. 'This book tells you about the most famous haunted houses in Sweden, but to be honest I'm not sure the one you mentioned is in there.'

Billie leafed through the pages. Most of the houses described in the book didn't even look like houses; they were more like palaces or castles.

'I think it might be better if you searched our archive of articles,' the assistant said. 'With a bit of luck some magazine or newspaper might have written about the house, and if that's the case, then I can help you get hold of the article.'

Billie thought that sounded like a good idea. They agreed that Simona would look at the book more carefully, while Billie and Aladdin checked out the archive.

The young man showed them to a computer, and they sat down.

'You can enter different search words here,' he said, pointing.

Billie and Aladdin looked at one another. They had no idea what to put.

'Try "haunted houses in Åhus",' Aladdin said, and Billie quickly typed the words into the box.

No matches.

'Try the street name,' the young man suggested.

Billie typed in Sparrisvägen and waited. The computer showed that there were ten articles in which Sparrisvägen was mentioned. Billie was excited.

'There you go,' the assistant said. 'I'll get those for you.'

He went off to look for the articles, and Billie and Aladdin went to sit with Simona.

'Have you found anything?' Billie asked.

'Look at this,' Simona said, pointing to the page she was reading.

The heading was *Mysteries in Åhus*, and the text was all about various houses in the area where the owners had insisted they were haunted. Billie gave a start when she was halfway down the page:

There are not very many haunted houses in Åhus, but one which experts definitively regard as being of interest is situated in the area known as Täppet. It is a small wooden structure where a young woman is said to have hanged herself in dubious circumstances a number of years ago. Rumour has it that the woman remained in the house after her death, and has malicious intentions towards all those who move in.

The house was used as a children's home in the 1920s, when it was known as Sunshine House. The woman who hanged herself worked as a children's nurse in the home.

Billie took a deep breath. Obviously they were talking about her house; this was almost exactly what Ella had told her and Aladdin. But Ella had said that it had been a school, not a children's home.

'Could she have got it wrong?' Billie said.

'Well, she is pretty old,' Aladdin said.

Billie read the section again. 'It doesn't say anything about the glass children,' she said with a sigh of disappointment.

The young man came back. 'The articles are

only available on microfilm,' he said. 'Do you know what that is?'

'No,' said Billie.

'It means you have to sit at a special machine in order to be able to read them. A microfilm is like a mini-photo which the machine enlarges, so that you can read the text on a screen. It's down in the basement if you want to have a go.'

Billie tucked the book about haunted houses under her arm and followed the young man downstairs. Aladdin and Simona sat down on either side of her in front of the screen. The man switched on the machine and showed them how to work it. It was a bit tricky at first, but once they had grasped what to do, it was pretty straightforward.

The first few articles they looked at had nothing whatsoever to do with Billie's house; they were about two families who had fallen out, missing cats, and other stuff that none of them wanted to read.

'There seems to be plenty going on where you live,' Simona joked as they looked at an article about a boy who had invented a new recipe for strawberry jam.

Aladdin changed the film so that they could read the remaining articles.

And there it was.

All three of them fell silent when they saw the picture next to the text. It was in black and white, but there was no doubt that it was Billie's house. It looked as if there had been a fire.

5 May 1940

Last night there was a serious fire at a house on Sparrisvägen in Åhus. At this stage the police are not prepared to reveal what they have discovered, but early indications suggest that the fire was a terrible accident. When the blaze took hold, there was a young couple in the house along with their son. The woman died in the flames, but her husband, Manne Lund, managed to save himself and his son. The boy escaped without injury, but is suffering from severe shock. It is not yet clear what will happen to the house.

So the house had been a children's home first of all, and then it had belonged to a family. And it wasn't only the girl who had hanged herself who had died there. Another person had lost her life in that house, but her husband and her child had survived. Imagine if they could track down either of them? They were bound to have lots of information about what had happened after the fire. Perhaps they even knew something about the glass children.

Chapter Twenty-Two

The house was filled with the smell of fried meatballs. Billie was sitting on her bed reading and Josef was busy cooking when the phone rang. Billie quickly dropped her book and ran downstairs to see if it was her mum.

'That's very kind of your parents, Aladdin,' Josef said. 'I was just frying meatballs, but we can easily have those tomorrow.'

He turned to Billie. 'Aladdin's parents have invited us to dinner at their restaurant this evening.'

Billie was delighted. Aladdin had taken her to

his parents' restaurant several times, but only because he needed something from his mum or dad; she had never eaten there.

Josef switched off the hob. 'Let's go,' he said.

Aladdin was waiting for them in the car park in front of the tower when they arrived on their bikes. His eyes were shining with excitement.

'Did you tell Josef what we found out at the library today?' he whispered as they followed Josef up the stairs to the restaurant.

'No,' Billie said.

She was afraid that Josef would get angry, just as her mum always did when she talked about ghosts in the house.

'I've been thinking,' Aladdin said. 'I believe there are at least two ghosts in your house – the girl who hanged herself, and the woman who died in the fire. Perhaps they're kind of fighting against one another. There might be a rule that says only one ghost is allowed to live in a house.'

Billie thought about it. That would mean that

the ghosts had a problem with each other, and not with Billie and her mum. But in that case, what was the explanation for everything that had happened recently?

'I think you could be right,' she whispered to Aladdin. 'But it definitely feels as if they want something from us – as if they're trying to get us out of the house.'

Aladdin looked serious. 'I'm just wondering why,' he said. 'What do they want the house for?'

The restaurant was small, with room for only a few customers. Billie knew that the kitchen was down at the bottom of the tower. She had heard Aladdin's mother say that the hardest thing was making sure the food didn't go cold before she got to the top of the long staircase.

'Are you missing your mum?' Josef said when they had sat down.

Billie nodded and swallowed. She missed her mum every minute of every hour.

'Me too,' Josef said.

They were sitting in silence when Aladdin brought the menus.

'Mum and Dad said you're to have whatever you want.'

Billie and Josef opened their menus and began to read, while Aladdin waited by their table.

'I think you should try the lamb,' he said.

'In that case, we will,' Josef said with a laugh, closing his menu. 'Then we can blame you if we don't like it.' He winked at Billie, and Aladdin disappeared.

'I've got something to tell you,' Josef said when they were alone. 'About your house.'

Billie was curious.

'I was speaking to a colleague about you and your mum today, and he knew exactly which house you lived in.'

'What?' Billie was shocked. 'Does he know someone who used to live there?'

'No. But he comes from Åhus, and he told me

163

some interesting things about the history of the house.'

Aladdin's mother arrived with a beer for Josef and a soft drink for Billie.

Billie leaned across the table so that she wouldn't miss a word that Josef said. 'And?' she said. 'What did he tell you?'

'Apparently your house used to be a children's home. Did you know that?'

Billie hesitated. Should she tell him what they had found out at the library? No, she daren't. Not yet.

'No,' she said. 'When was that?'

'A long time ago – in the 1920s, according to my colleague. 1920 to 1922, I think. The council built the house for the children.'

'1920 to 1922? That's not very long. What happened?'

'I don't know,' Josef said. 'My colleague wasn't sure.'

Although she couldn't explain why, Billie had a

feeling that this business of the house having been a children's home was important, something that might go some way towards explaining all the terrible things that had happened.

Why had the children's home existed for such a short time? Did it have something to do with the glass children? Billie decided that she would try to find out more the very next day. They would go back to the library and try some fresh searches.

Aladdin's mother appeared with two large plates. 'Lamb,' she said. 'Skåne's finest. Enjoy.'

The food smelled absolutely delicious, and Billie tucked in with relish.

Next summer would be different. By then she and her mum would have moved back to Kristianstad. The first step was to find out what was wrong with the house, and the next was to persuade her mum that they had to leave.

When they had finished their meal, Aladdin's father came over to say hello. Josef asked how long the family had been living in Sweden, and Billie took the opportunity to slip away to the loo. When she came out, she heard a voice behind her.

'So you're still in Åhus.'

Billie turned round quickly. It was Ella, the old lady. She smiled at Billie, but then her expression grew serious.

'Have you spoken to your mother yet?' she asked.

Billie shook her head. 'I have to find out more before I speak to her,' she said. 'So that I can be sure she'll listen to me.'

Ella gazed at Billie. 'That's probably a sensible approach,' she said. 'Just remember that you don't have much time. Think about what's happened to everyone else who's lived in that house.'

Billie looked over at Josef. He was still talking to Aladdin's father.

'I have to go,' she said.

'Good luck,' said Ella.

Billie hurried back to Josef. She didn't want to tell Ella that her mum had been taken ill and rushed to hospital in an ambulance. That something bad had already happened to them.

Ella was right. Billie really didn't have much time left to save herself and her mum.

Chapter Twenty-Three

Only Billie and Simona went back to the library the following day. Aladdin had a piano lesson, and wouldn't have time to get into Kristianstad before the library closed.

'Call me this evening and tell me what you've found out!' he said when Billie spoke to him in the morning.

'Will do,' Billie said.

Full of anticipation, she and Simona sat down at the same computer as last time and tried some new searches in the archive of articles, using the name 'Sunshine House'. To their disappointment, they didn't get as many matches as they had hoped.

'Try "children's home" and "Åhus" instead,' Simona suggested.

But it made no difference.

'That's funny,' Billie said with a frown.

They went to the information desk to ask for help in accessing the small number of articles they had found. It was the same young man who had helped them last time.

'You ought to try the museum when you've finished here,' he said as he searched for the right microfilm. 'They're running an exhibition at the moment about childcare in Skåne during the twentieth century. They might know something about the children's home you're interested in.'

The museum? Simona and Billie looked at one another and nodded. Good idea. Billie glanced at her watch, hoping they would have time to get everything done before Josef came to pick her up. They also had to call and see Mum at the hospital on the way home.

Billie was very pleased to discover that even though there weren't many articles, she was able to learn a great deal from them. The first one was about the opening of the children's home.

3 October 1920

Herr Green, the master builder who was responsible for the construction of the children's home, attended a lunch held at the residence of the county governor. Herr Persson, the chairman of the council, thanked herr Green for his work. The children's home is in the Täppet district of Åhus, and the aim is to give orphaned children a secure place in which to live. The home is expected to have room for at least eight children, and has been named Sunshine House.

'Eight children,' Simona said, her eyes widening as she read the article. 'Can you really fit that many people in your house?'

'They must have slept in bunk beds, with

several children in each room,' said Billie, who had been thinking exactly the same thing. 'The staff might have slept in the spare room next to the kitchen.'

'Even so, it must have been a bit of a squash,' Simona said. 'I mean, there's loads of us in my family, but we've all got our own room.'

Billie didn't know anyone who lived in a house as big as Simona's. Her parents had bought and renovated an old farmhouse so they'd have enough space for all their children.

The next article provided more information about the children's home, giving details about how big it was and what kind of children would be living there. The council wanted disabled children to be given priority.

They moved on to the final article on their list.

3 August 1922
Today the council decided to close the Sunshine House children's home in Åhus after the extremely

tragic events reported in this newspaper last week. The governing body will decide what to do with the house later this autumn.

Both Billie and Simona read the article over and over again. *After the extremely tragic events* . . . What events? Why hadn't they found an article about whatever had happened?

Billie could feel her heart pounding harder and harder. They were close now, she could feel it. Soon she would know what secrets the house was brooding on. Soon, soon, soon.

She leaped up from her chair and tugged at Simona's arm. 'Come on!' she said. 'Let's go to the museum!'

The museum in Kristianstad was on the main square. Billie had been there with her school in the past, but never under her own steam.

'I hate museums,' Simona said as they walked in.

Billie quite liked them sometimes, but she didn't say so. She was glad that Simona had come along even though she thought it was boring.

But where should they start?

'Here!' Simona said, pointing to a sign.

NEW EXHIBITION:

CHILDCARE IN KRISTIANSTAD DURING

THE 20TH CENTURY

Billie looked at her watch. It was four o'clock. Josef was picking her up at five outside the library so that they could go to the hospital. She had to be there in time.

They quickly headed for the exhibition room, and Billie gasped. So many pictures and artefacts. There were lots and lots of small models of houses and other buildings.

'Help,' Simona sighed. 'This is going to take for ever.'

She was absolutely right. And what were they actually looking for?

'Maybe we can ask her for help?' Billie said, pointing to a young girl who was walking around the room.

They hurried over to her.

'Excuse me,' Simona said. 'Do you work here?'

'Yes,' said the girl. 'How can I help?'

She seemed pleased to see them. There were hardly any other visitors at the moment.

'We were wondering if you knew anything about a children's home called Sunshine House? It was in Åhus in the 1920s,' Billie said.

The girl's expression grew serious. 'Indeed I do,' she said. 'What was it you wanted to know?'

Everything, Billie thought. 'My friend and I have to write something for school about how orphaned children were looked after long ago,' she said. 'And somebody mentioned Sunshine House.'

'Billie's only just moved to Åhus,' Simona added. 'So we thought it would be interesting to write about a children's home that used to be there.'

Billie looked at the girl's badge; her name was Amanda.

'I understand,' she said. 'Unfortunately Sunshine House isn't included in this exhibition, but I actually wrote an essay about that particular children's home when I was at university. It's a terrible story, but then I'm sure you know that already.'

Billie and Simona exchanged a glance.

'Mmm,' said Billie. 'But we'd really like to find out exactly what happened.'

'In that case I think we should go and sit on the sofa over there, and I'll tell you all about it,' Amanda said.

Chapter Twenty-Four

Perhaps Billie should have realized that her house was sitting on a very dark secret. That she was about to hear a truly dreadful story. But when Amanda started to tell them about Sunshine House, Billie was lost for words. Even Simona, who loved to talk, was struck dumb.

'The children's home was indeed called Sunshine House, just as you said,' Amanda began. 'But no one ever referred to it as anything but the Glass House. Did you know that?'

Billie shook her head. 'Why did they call it the

Glass House?' she said, and realized that she was whispering.

'Because five of the eight children who lived there were glass children.'

Glass children? At last they were going to find out!

'Glass children was the name given to those born with severe brittle bone disease,' Amanda explained. 'It is still regarded as a serious illness, but in those days it wasn't possible to do very much for children with that particular disability. They needed constant supervision to stop them from falling and hurting themselves. Do you know what brittle bone disease is?'

'I think so,' Simona said. 'It means you break your arms and legs more easily than other people.'

'Exactly,' Amanda said. 'There are various kinds of brittle bone disease, and not all of them are equally severe. But sometimes it's very bad, and it can even mean that a person doesn't grow

177

properly. The children who lived in the Glass House, or Sunshine House, all had different major problems, but a number of them were seriously ill.'

Billie tried to imagine what it would be like to have that kind of illness, knowing that you could break your arms or legs if you just tripped over. So awful.

Glass children.

It was a good description of children who suffered from brittle bone disease.

'As you know, there were eight children, and they were looked after by two women. One was in charge of the home, and the other was a young children's nurse called Majken.'

Amanda fell silent, and Billie thought she wasn't going to say any more. But she had just paused for a moment, and went on:

'In practice Majken was the one who actually took care of the children, and as you can imagine it was a difficult job for just one person, particularly in view of the fact that several of the children were ill. The summer of 1922 was a very bad summer, with lots of rain. But in August the weather improved, and it was hot and sunny. One day when Majken was alone with all the children, she decided to take them down to the beach. Those who were healthy helped out by pulling the sick children along in little carts, and in that way Majken managed to get all the children down to the sea.'

It was hard to imagine what it must have looked like, but Billie did her best. Sparrisvägen would have been no more than a dirt track back then, and the dust would have whirled up around the carts. And it must have been hard work too, even if it wasn't very far to the sea.

'They left the home at ten o'clock in the morning,' Amanda continued. 'They settled down on the beach known as Kantarellen today. Don't ask me how she managed to control the glass children. Perhaps she made sure they stayed sitting on blankets under a parasol. The healthy children were allowed to run around, playing and paddling in the sea.'

Just as Billie herself had done during the summer. Once again she pictured Majken and the eight children.

'The beach was different in those days,' Amanda said. 'The sandy area was wider, and the sea wasn't as shallow as it is now, especially not when it was windy and the water was choppy. And the day Majken took the children down to the sea all by herself, it was very windy indeed.'

Suddenly Billie felt a pain in her stomach. She wasn't sure she wanted to hear any more about Majken and the glass children, but Amanda carried on with her story.

'There weren't many other people on the beach, but several witnesses saw what happened. The wind must have grown stronger, because the waves got bigger and bigger, and suddenly there was the sound of screaming from the sea.

Without Majken noticing, two of the children with brittle bone disease had gone into the water and been knocked off their feet by the waves. Majken ran straight in, but the current dragged the children further and further out, and she had to struggle to make any progress. When she did reach them, it was already too late. They had been under the water for too long, and they had both drowned.'

'How awful,' Simona whispered.

'Indeed it was,' Amanda said. 'Majken pulled them ashore, and of course there was a police investigation.'

'But why?' Billie asked.

'To find out whether Majken had failed in her duty of care, as it was called. They reached the conclusion that she should never have gone to the beach on her own with so many children, but they also stated that she shouldn't have been left in charge by herself in the first place. Therefore she was not punished, and because the children were so fond of her, she was allowed to remain at the home as a children's nurse.'

The tears came from nowhere, and Billie blinked several times to get rid of them. If Amanda noticed that she was about to cry, she would stop talking.

'What happened?' Simona said.

Amanda glanced at Billie. 'I'm not sure you can cope with any more.'

'Of course we can!' Billie and Simona said in unison.

'Where was I?' Amanda said. 'Oh yes, Majken escaped any kind of punishment. And she returned to the home as a nurse, even though she must have been feeling absolutely terrible about what had happened. The council started to wonder whether it had been such a good idea to set up the children's home in the first place, and there was a debate in the local paper about the best way to take care of orphaned children. But only a week later, something happened that changed everything.'

Billie was holding her breath.

'Majken just couldn't live with the guilt she felt over the two children who had drowned. One night she got out of bed, went into the living room at the home and unhooked the ceiling light. And then . . .'

Billie knew what was coming, and her heart was pounding so hard that it must surely be visible through her top.

'. . . she hanged herself,' Amanda continued. 'The manageress found her the following morning, before the children woke up. Sunshine House was closed just a few weeks later, and the children were sent elsewhere.'

Simona placed a hand on Billie's arm. 'So now we know who she was, the girl who died in the house,' she said quietly.

Amanda got to her feet. 'I'm worried you might have nightmares after hearing such a sad story,' she said, looking as if she was about to leave.

'No, it's fine,' Billie reassured her. 'We wanted to hear it. I don't suppose you know what happened to the house afterwards, when it wasn't a children's home any more?'

Amanda frowned. 'It was empty for many years. Then a family moved in, but there was a fire.'

That was exactly what Ella had said – that things turned out badly for everyone who had lived there.

Billie had one last question on her mind, and in the end she just had to ask. 'I don't suppose you've heard anything about the house being haunted?' she said, feeling her cheeks flush red.

Amanda turned away so that she wasn't looking at Billie or Simona; it was as if she was avoiding eye contact. 'Yes,' she said slowly. 'I have. Some people say that Majken still haunts the place. That it doesn't matter what kind of lamp you put up in the living room, it always swings to and fro as if someone were hanging from it. And I've heard another story too.'

About the woman who burned to death, Billie thought.

But that wasn't what Amanda said at all.

'About the glass children who drowned. It's said that they wanted to come back home, that they couldn't find peace when they died. They wanted to return to the children's home, and so they drive away everyone who moves into the house on Sparrisvägen.'

At that moment Billie remembered the handprint in the dust that she had found just after she and her mum moved to Åhus. The little print of a child's hand.

And she realized that they could have been wrong. Perhaps it was neither Majken nor the woman who had burned to death who haunted their house. Perhaps it was the children who had once lived there, and wanted to come home.

Chapter Twenty-Five

It had started to rain by the time Josef parked outside the hospital.

'You're very quiet,' he said as he switched off the engine. 'How did you get on today? Did you find out anything about the children's home?'

'Not much,' Billie said evasively.

Her mind was whirling after everything she had heard. She must call Aladdin as soon as she got home. They had to talk about everything that had happened, and what to do next. She had no intention of saying anything to Josef before that, and she definitely wasn't going to tell her mum.

Mum was much better. She was sitting up in bed having something to eat when Josef and Billie arrived, and she gave Billie a big hug. Her arms felt just as strong as they always did, and Billie could tell from her eyes that she wasn't so ill any more. She wasn't tired and confused as she had been over the past few days. She talked and laughed several times when Billie and Josef told her what they had been doing.

'The doctor says I can come home at the weekend,' she said, stroking Billie's cheek. 'Isn't that wonderful?'

'Mmm,' Billie said.

At the weekend. Before then, she and Aladdin and Simona would have worked out how to get Billie and her mum out of that house. Somehow.

'It'll be so nice to sleep in my own bed,' Mum said. 'To get back to our little house.'

She smiled warmly at Billie, who forced herself to smile back. Soon she would have to talk to her mum about the house, but not right now.

In the car on the way back to Åhus, Billie thought about the glass children all the time.

'Wow!' Aladdin said when Billie had finished telling him her story on the phone. 'So the ghosts in your house are children, not adults.'

'So it seems,' Billie said.

But she couldn't help having her doubts. Did ghosts really exist? Hadn't they talked about this, and decided that they didn't? But if ghosts didn't exist, then how had a child's handprint appeared in the dust on the table in the spare room?

Aladdin agreed with her. At the moment, the idea that the house was haunted was the best explanation they had for everything that had happened.

'Perhaps we could try to speak to the ghosts, if they do exist?' Billie said slowly. 'You know, ask them what they want?'

Aladdin snorted. 'My mum believes in that kind of stuff, but I think it's just rubbish. Speak to the ghosts? I mean, if it is down to them that everyone who lives in that house comes off badly, then I don't really see the point in speaking to them. Surely that means they're just nasty?'

On the one hand Billie agreed, but on the other, she didn't. Perhaps the ghosts were responsible for the spooky stuff – the tapping on the windows, the handprint in the dust and so on – while the accidents were simply accidents?

'Is there anyone else we can ask?' Billie wondered. 'Shouldn't we try to get hold of the father and son who survived the house fire? They seem to have been the first family to move in after the children's home was closed down.'

'But what can they tell us?' Aladdin said doubtfully. 'They might not even be alive any longer.'

'You obviously can't count,' Billie said wearily. 'The father is probably dead, or at least very, very old, but the son would be no more than seventy or eighty now.'

Seventy wasn't all that old. Not if you were fit and healthy, like Grandma and Grandpa, for example. Sometimes Billie thought those two would go on for ever.

'OK, but how do we find him?' Aladdin said. 'We don't even know his name, just that his father was called Manne Lund.'

'I could ask Josef for help,' Billie said.

She looked at the copies of the articles she had brought home from the library. *Manne Lund*. That must be quite an unusual name.

'Why Josef?'

'Well, he works for the police. They're usually pretty good at tracking people down,' Billie said.

She curled up on her bed, the telephone pressed against her ear. Josef was busy in the kitchen, and she could hear him opening and closing cupboard doors. Billie's dad had never enjoyed cooking or baking, but Josef was different. He seemed to be more like Aladdin's dad – he couldn't get enough of being in the kitchen. If Josef got fed up with being a police officer, perhaps he could open a restaurant too.

Then Billie thought of someone else who they needed to talk to. Someone who ought to know a great deal. And who had a lot of explaining to do.

'There's someone else,' she said.

'Who's that?' Aladdin asked.

'Martin.'

'Who?' Aladdin sounded surprised.

'The man who showed me and Mum around the house when we bought it. The man who told us so many lies.'

Billie remembered exactly what Martin had looked like on the day he met them outside the house. She remembered how he had led the way up the steps and shown them around. How he had avoided answering some of their questions, and how he had contradicted himself. This time he wouldn't get away with it so easily.

'Perhaps we should start by speaking to him after school tomorrow,' Aladdin suggested. 'And we can ask Josef whether he can find out any more about Manne Lund or his son.'

That sounded like a good idea. When Billie had finished talking to Aladdin, she called Simona, then went downstairs to speak to Josef. Unlike her mum, he didn't ask a lot of questions, so Billie felt slightly ashamed of herself when she said she had to track down Manne Lund for a school project. She had given the same explanation at the library and the museum, and nobody seemed to think it was odd. Nor did Josef.

'Just write down what you already know, and I'll check it out tomorrow,' he said.

All she had to do now was track down Martin's address, and that wasn't difficult. Mum had asked for his contact details when they moved in, and the piece of paper was still on the notice board in the hallway.

Josef settled down in front of the TV after

dinner, and Billie slipped into the hallway and took down the piece of paper. It crossed her mind again that it was a long time since she had seen or heard anything strange in the house. Everything had been quiet since her mum was taken ill, as if whatever had frightened Billie thought the fact that her mum had contracted meningitis was enough for the time being.

Billie glanced over at the spare room. The door was closed. The worst things had happened inside that room; it was several days since Billie had been in there.

Hesitantly she moved across to the closed door and placed her hand on the handle. There was no need to be afraid now; it wasn't night time, and Josef was in the room next door. But her hand was still trembling slightly as she opened the door. Cautiously she stepped inside. It had a musty smell.

She let out a long breath when she switched on the light and saw that everything was as it should be. Even the little table, the one she had liked so much at first, looked fine. No messages, no handprints.

Then she looked over at the window and turned to a block of ice where she stood. Several times she made herself close her eyes and open them again. But no, there was no mistake. She was panting with fear and astonishment.

The windowsill was not empty. There was something there that shouldn't be there.

Someone had placed the glass children in the window.

Chapter Twenty-Six

It was blowing a gale when Billie collected her bike and cycled over to Aladdin's after school the following day. He was waiting for her on the pavement outside his house with a map in his hand.

'It's not far,' he said. 'It'll only take a few minutes to cycle there.'

Billie thought that was just as well, because the sky was ominously grey, and it looked as if it might start pouring with rain at any moment.

'Did you speak to Josef?' Aladdin said. 'Has he found Manne Lund and his son?'

'I don't know,' Billie said. 'I'll ask him when he gets home from work.'

However, she had no intention of telling Josef about the glass children in the window. She had told Aladdin and Simona, but no one else. The risk of not being believed was too great.

Billie felt guilty because she had gone straight to Åhus on the bus after school instead of calling in to see her mum as she usually did. But the house was dangerous. That was all there was to it. And that was why Billie had to find out as much as possible, so that she could persuade her mum that they had to move.

Martin lived in a white wooden house with red eaves. Just as Billie and Aladdin turned into the garden, the first drops of rain began to fall. They quickly dropped their bikes and ran up onto the veranda to ring the doorbell.

They rang twice. The rain was pattering on the roof, and Billie shivered in her summer jacket.

'What if he's not home?' Aladdin said.

'He has to be,' Billie replied, banging on the door.

They heard footsteps on the other side and waited anxiously as someone fiddled with the lock. The door opened slowly, and Martin was standing there.

Even though Billie hadn't seen him since the day he showed them around the house, she recognized him immediately. But he looked so tired! And had he really been so old the last time she saw him? He must have been, of course, but Billie thought he looked older now.

Martin looked at her with weary eyes, and nodded slowly. 'I recognize you,' he said. 'How are you getting on in the house?'

'Fine, thanks,' Billie said. 'This is my friend Aladdin. We were wondering if you had time for a little chat.'

Aladdin said hello politely and shook hands, and Martin took a step backwards.

'I've always got time,' he said. 'Come on in.'

Martin's house reminded Billie of their house on Sparrisvägen, with small rooms on two floors. But Martin had really nice wallpaper and newer furniture.

'How have things been?' Martin said. 'Did you manage to sell your house in town?'

Billie swallowed. 'Not yet, what with the summer holidays and everything. But the agent doesn't think it will take much longer.'

She would have preferred to say that they had no intention of selling their house in town, because they would be leaving Åhus soon, never to return. But instead she followed Martin into his living room, where they sat down at a large dining table. Billie couldn't see any photographs of a wife or children, which made her feel sad. Martin looked about the same age as her grand-parents, and they would have been terribly lonely if they didn't have one another.

'What was it you wanted to know?' Martin said.

Aladdin looked at Billie.

'We've got one or two questions about the house on Sparrisvägen,' Billie said in a small voice.

'Oh yes?' Martin said, suddenly sounding annoyed.

He leaned back and folded his arms the way Billie had seen lots of adults do when they were cross. 'What's on your mind?' he said.

Suddenly everything felt so wrong. What were they actually doing here?

'Well,' Billie said even more quietly. 'We were wondering whether you knew why so many families have chosen not to stay in the house?'

She was surprised to hear her own voice asking such a brave question. Straight to the point, as Dad would have said.

Martin stared at her for a long time before he answered. 'What do you mean?' he said.

The palms of Billie's hands suddenly felt damp, and she wiped them on her jeans. Why was he being so difficult?

She plucked up courage once more. 'The last family only lived in the house for a year or so, and we've found out that several other families have done the same – they've moved out after a very short time.'

'We've also heard that the families moved out because people got hurt in that house,' Aladdin said, sounding quite cocky.

Martin sighed. 'So that's what you've heard, is it?'

He spread his hands wide and sighed again, as if he thought they were incredibly stupid. 'I've also heard a lot of gossip about the house on Sparrisvägen, but to be honest I don't believe a word of it. After all, people move for all kinds of reasons. Thinking there's something wrong with the house itself is just ridiculous.'

However, Billie had no intention of giving up.

She knew that Martin had already lied about several things.

'How long had the house been empty when Mum and I moved in?'

'A year, just as I told you the last time you asked,' Martin said calmly.

'But that's not true,' Billie said; she couldn't help getting cross. 'We've spoken to several people, and we know that the family who lived there actually moved out two years ago.'

Martin didn't say a word; he just sat there at the table staring at them.

'We know that you lied about the furniture too,' Aladdin said. 'You said it belonged to the previous owners, but that's not true. That furniture is really old.'

Billie waited for Martin to give in and admit that he hadn't told them the truth. With a bit of luck he would also tell them why he had lied. But still he said nothing – he just looked even more angry. Billie noticed that he was clenching his fists so tightly that his knuckles had gone white.

'Get out of my house with your nonsense!' Martin snapped, and even though he wasn't shouting, Billie knew that it was time to leave before he exploded.

She and Aladdin got to their feet at the same time and practically ran to the door. Behind them they could hear Martin's voice:

'Get out!' he yelled. 'Get out and leave me alone!'

They had never cycled so fast in their lives. They didn't stop until they reached Billie's house. It was pouring with rain, but that was the least of their worries.

'Goodness,' Aladdin said when they were curled up on the sofa in the living room under a blanket each. 'Did you buy the house from him? He seems a bit . . . odd.'

Billie couldn't help but agree. She had been so scared when Martin started shouting. Why had he done that? Why didn't he just talk to them, tell them what he knew? Because he knew something, she was sure of it.

'I don't know why Mum trusted him,' she mumbled into her blanket. 'I never liked him.'

Aladdin shuffled further into his corner of the sofa and rested his head on the back. 'I hope things go better when we speak to Manne Lund,' he said.

'They couldn't go much worse,' Billie said, and started to giggle.

The giggle turned into loud laughter, and it was catching. Aladdin started to laugh too, and they laughed and laughed until they couldn't breathe as they thought about how they had gone to see a man they didn't know and tried to get him to tell them his secrets.

They were laughing so hard that they didn't hear Josef unlock the door and walk in.

'Hello, you two,' he said, smiling when he saw them on the sofa.

Billie and Aladdin were so surprised that they stopped laughing.

Josef went into the kitchen with a bag of shopping. 'Would you like to stay for tea?' he said to Aladdin.

'Yes please!'

They had already decided that if Josef had found a phone number for Manne Lund or his son, they would ring that very evening.

Billie stumbled into the kitchen with the blanket tightly wrapped around her body. 'Did you find him?' she asked. 'Manne Lund, I mean? Is he still alive?'

Josef was putting a carton of milk in the fridge. 'I think so,' he said. 'There weren't many men with that name who were the right sort of age. I've brought the address and phone number. Unfortunately I wasn't able to find out whether he had any children, and if so what their names are.'

Billie tried not to look too pleased as he took a piece of paper out of his pocket.

'Brilliant, thanks!' she said.

The Manne Lund Josef had found lived in Malmö, and was almost a hundred years old.

'Just bear in mind when you call him that he might not be the right person,' Josef cautioned. 'The Manne you're looking for could well be dead.'

Billie knew that, but still she had a strong feeling that this was the right man. Manne Lund had lived in her house. He must know a great deal. She just hoped he wasn't senile and confused, given how old he was. If that was the case, he wouldn't be able to tell them much at all.

'We'll be eating in half an hour,' Josef said. 'Could you and Aladdin set the table, please?'

Billie did as he asked. First they would have tea, then they would call Manne. And then Billie hoped they would have the information they needed to convince Mum that they had to move out.

Because time was short now. Shorter than it

had ever been. After the visit to Martin, Billie was absolutely certain: there was something dangerous in this house, and there had to be someone who knew what it was all about.

Chapter Twenty-Seven

'The glass children,' Aladdin said.

They had bolted their food then raced up to Billie's room, where they were now sitting and talking quietly.

'You think this is all about the glass children who died?' Billie said.

'Yes, and about the girl who hanged herself in the living room – Majken.'

'But what do they want?'

'Who?'

'The ghosts.'

Aladdin was fiddling with a book on the

bedside table. 'What if there aren't any ghosts?' he said slowly.

Billie was confused. 'I thought we both believed the same thing – that the ghosts were causing all the problems. That's what you said, like, two seconds ago!'

Aladdin shook his head. 'I think everything that has happened is to do with the glass children and Majken,' he said. 'But this business of ghosts . . . I've been thinking about it a lot ever since you told me about those glass figures on the windowsill. Do ghosts really do that kind of thing?'

'But who else could it be?' Billie said, slightly louder than she had intended. 'Who would be able to get into the house without us noticing, and do weird stuff like putting out comics, leaving messages and arranging glass figures?'

'Someone with a key. Just as we thought right at the start, when neither of us believed in ghosts.'

'And who would that be?'

'Just think about it. This is an old house, and loads of different people have lived here. Did you change the locks when you moved in?'

Billie shook her head. No, they hadn't changed the locks.

'So you think one of the former owners has kept a key, and is creeping around here day and night just to scare me?' Billie said doubtfully.

Aladdin's expression grew serious. 'Does a ghost sound more likely? Be honest, Billie. Does it?'

Billie looked away. She didn't know what to think any more.

Manne's voice sounded really old. Sometimes Billie had to press the phone right against her ear so that she could hear him. However, he wasn't in the least confused, and seem pleased that someone had called him.

'To think that that house is still causing

problems,' he sighed when Billie explained why she had rung him.

Billie looked at Aladdin, who was sitting right next to her on the bed trying to hear what Manne was saying. They had closed the door of her bedroom for privacy.

'I read an old newspaper article about a fire,' Billie began cautiously.

She didn't know how the old man would react. He might get very upset when he was reminded of the fire.

'That's right,' he said. 'My wife died, but my son and I survived.'

Manne didn't sound particularly distressed, so Billie ventured a few more questions. Perhaps it was so long ago that it didn't hurt to talk about it any more.

'What happened to the house after the fire?' she asked.

Manne sighed. He probably was a bit sad after all.

'The boy and I moved to Malmö. I couldn't afford to fix up the house in Åhus, so it just stood there. The neighbours complained, of course. They didn't want a burned-out building next door. But I didn't care.'

'So you sold the house?' Billie said.

'No, I didn't. I left it standing there for over fifteen years, and then my son moved back to Åhus to work as a fisherman. I signed the house over to him on the understanding that he would renovate it and rebuild the parts that had been damaged by the fire.'

So after the fire the house had just stood there rotting for more than fifteen years before anyone bothered with it. If Billie had been a ghost, she would have been angry too.

'Did your son live in the house, or did he sell it?' she asked.

For the first time Manne seemed hesitant. Eventually he said: 'He sold it. But . . . the thing is, my son was never really himself after the fire.

Even though he was so young when his mother died, I think he went a little bit funny that night. He still thinks the house is haunted.'

Billie thought he wasn't the only one.

'Did he ever mention dead children?' she said.

'Are you thinking about the glass children, the ones who drowned?' Manne said. 'Yes, he talked about them. He claimed that they didn't want anyone else to live in the house, and that they were the ones who had set fire to it. But . . . that was complete nonsense. The fire started because I was careless with the fire in the stove that night. And those dead children . . .'

Billie waited, holding her breath.

'Well, what can you say? Their deaths were a terrible accident, but to say that they are still here in our world, among those of us who are living and breathing – no, I don't believe that. I mean, that's like saying they became evil when they died, and that's just so stupid it's ridiculous.'

It sounded so sensible when Manne put it like

that. Why should those children have turned nasty when they died? Why would they make people sick and unhappy, just because they wanted the house for themselves? It was, exactly as Manne said, a really stupid idea.

He was beginning to sound tired. Billie realized that she didn't have much time left. He would soon want to end the call.

'So if it isn't the children who are haunting the place, why have so many bad things happened to people in this house?' she asked.

Manne couldn't possibly know the answer, but it would be interesting to hear what he thought.

Manne coughed down the phone, and for a while Billie wasn't sure if he was going to answer. Eventually he said: 'They say that the girl who hanged herself has come back as a ghost, and that she drives people away. But I don't believe that either. I think it's a coincidence, something that just happens. My beloved son is still afraid of the house you live in, but that's just foolish. There is nothing to be afraid of. Not if you don't believe in ghosts, which I certainly don't.'

Billie got quite excited. 'So your son is still afraid of the house?' she said. 'Has he moved away from Åhus, or does he still live here?'

'Oh, he'll never move away,' Manne said. 'He's retired now, but he'll never leave Åhus. It wouldn't surprise me if he's still keeping an eye on your house even now, he was so obsessed with the place.'

'What do you mean?' Billie said.

There was another burst of coughing at the other end of the line, and the sound of running water in the background. Manne was probably having a drink to try to get rid of the cough.

'As I said, he went a bit funny when his mother died. When he went back to Åhus and rebuilt the house, he got the idea that it had to look exactly the way it did when we bought it. The previous owners had left behind lots of old furniture which I stored in the cellar when we moved in. It had belonged to the children's home, and both my wife and I thought everything was too old and grubby. When my son returned to Åhus and renovated the house, he dug out all those antiquated pieces and sold the place furnished. It was a way of keeping the glass children away, he insisted. If the house looked exactly the same as it used to do, they wouldn't be as displeased.'

Billie heard Manne laughing quietly to himself.

'Can you imagine anything more ridiculous?' he said.

Billie wasn't so sure. Because now she realized where all the old furniture in the house had come from. A new idea began to take shape in her mind, and when she asked the next question her voice was no more than a whisper.

'What's your son's name?'

Manne answered equally quietly.

And suddenly Billie started to understand how everything hung together.

When she had ended the call she turned to Aladdin and said: 'Now I know who's been haunting this house.'

Chapter Twenty-Eight

During the night following Billie's conversation with Manne Lund, it absolutely poured with rain. She lay awake for a long time listening to the heavy drops hammering on the roof, but she still didn't feel tired when she got up in the morning.

'I'll get the bus to school today,' she said to Josef. 'We've got a late start – I don't have to be in until ten o'clock.'

Josef looked surprised and glanced at her timetable, which was stuck on the fridge.

'No you haven't,' he said.

'Yes we have – Maths is cancelled because our

teacher has a doctor's appointment. He'll be back for English at ten.'

Billie wasn't a good liar, but right now she was lying as if she'd never done anything else in her entire life.

Josef still looked doubtful. 'Don't you have a supply teacher when someone's away?'

'Not when it's only a couple of lessons. If you don't believe me, why don't you ring the school and check?' she said, trying to sound slightly annoyed.

'Of course I believe you!' Josef said. 'Are you sure you're happy to go on the bus? Otherwise I can always go into work a bit later – it's no problem.'

Oh please, please, just go! Billie thought.

Josef put on his shoes and jacket and slipped his work bag over his shoulder. 'Tomorrow afternoon we can pick up your mum and bring her home, OK?' he said with a smile.

Billie nodded. It was definitely OK. Everything was going to be fine. Everything.

As soon as Josef had driven off, Billie left the house. She was wearing her jacket and rucksack exactly as if she was going to school. Her hand shook as she turned the key, then cycled off towards the bus stop. If anyone saw her they would assume she was going to catch the bus to school.

But she wasn't. Aladdin was waiting for her in the trees behind the bus stop.

'Did anyone see you?' he said.

'I don't think so,' Billie replied.

A little while later the bus from Kristianstad pulled up on the other side of the road and Simona got off. As soon as she had joined them, they set off back towards Billie's house.

It was now or never; they were going to unmask the ghost. They were going to catch it red-handed.

*   *   *

The plan was Billie's, and it was very simple. They would keep the house under surveillance all day, waiting until the 'ghost' tried to get in without anyone noticing. They would then try to talk some sense into the 'ghost', and if that didn't work they would call Josef and ask him for help.

Billie was so nervous that she had a pain in her tummy. It was a good job there were three of them.

'How do we know the ghost will turn up today?' Simona said.

'We don't,' Aladdin replied. 'But with a bit of luck, it will. Otherwise we'll have to think again.'

Each of them had managed to avoid going to school that morning, using different ways and means, and it felt both exciting and scary. Before leaving home, Billie had called the school and said that she wouldn't be coming in because she had to go and visit her mum in hospital. Her teacher knew that Billie's mum was ill, and was immediately concerned. Had her mum taken a turn for the worse? Billie felt really bad when she said yes, her mum was a little worse, and that was why Billie wanted to be with her.

'Wouldn't it be good if you and your mum could stay in Åhus when we've unmasked the ghost?' Aladdin had said the previous evening when they were sitting on Billie's bed, planning what to do.

Billie hadn't known what to say. It wasn't just because of the ghost that she wanted to move back to Kristianstad. There were so many other reasons – her friends, that kind of thing. Or was there a chance that she might be able to settle in Åhus? Could she be happy living here?

That was too big a question, and it would have to wait until they had unmasked the ghost. Only then would she know what she wanted.

They approached Billie's house through the grove of pine trees on the other side of the road. The trees were close enough together to provide a good hiding place. Billie had left her bike at the bus stop. She opened her rucksack and took out her dad's old binoculars. They were some distance from the house, but with the binoculars they could see quite clearly. Simona had brought a small telescope.

'Cool,' Aladdin said, his voice full of admiration.

Simona smiled.

They sat down on the ground on picnic blankets they had brought with them; all three had also packed plenty to eat. Billie was happy as long as it didn't rain, but she wished it was a bit less windy and that the sky wasn't quite so grey. It would be cold sitting here hiding among the trees all day if the sun didn't come out.

After only an hour or so Billie decided she was getting quite uncomfortable sitting on the ground, and stood up. She handed the binoculars to Aladdin while she stretched her legs. The only sound was the birds, flying from tree to tree.

What if the ghost didn't come? They couldn't sit here day after day. And tomorrow Mum would be home, which meant Billie could forget any further attempts at bunking off school. On the other hand, Mum would be signed off work for several weeks; the ghost was bound to stay away while she was at home.

Billie shivered and stamped her feet up and down. How come it was so cold? It had been summer not so long ago!

'Look!' Aladdin hissed excitedly, and Billie immediately sat down.

'What's happening?' Simona whispered, looking through her telescope.

Billie reached for her binoculars, but Aladdin wouldn't give them back.

'I can't see anything out of the ordinary,' Simona said.

Aladdin started giggling, and passed the binoculars to Billie. 'Neither can I – I just wanted to check that you two were awake,' he said.

Simona burst out laughing as well, and Billie playfully hit Aladdin on the arm. 'Pack it in,' she said, trying not to laugh.

Then they settled down quietly among the trees and carried on waiting.

It started to rain, and they got out their raincoats. After a while it stopped, but the sky had changed from grey to black, and Billie was afraid they might be in for a thunderstorm. If that happened they might have to give up and go indoors.

There was another shower, then it stopped again. Aladdin announced that he was hungry, so they all had a sandwich. Then they waited again, taking turns with the binoculars and the telescope. Billie had an apple for dessert, and a rabbit hopped past their hiding place. Billie was starting to feel tired, and so were her two friends.

There'll be no ghost hunt today, she thought. *It was a stupid idea right from the start. How could we possibly think it would work?*

Then she heard Aladdin whisper: 'Quick – look!'

She could tell from his voice that he was serious. Her stomach tied itself in knots, and she could hardly breathe as she looked over towards the house. Someone was walking up the steps.

'Give me the binoculars!' she hissed.

Reluctantly Aladdin handed them over.

And it was true. Someone was standing on the patio fiddling with the lock. The door swung open, and the ghost went inside. Even though it was raining again, Billie could see that she had been right.

Martin, the man who had shown Billie and her mum around the house, was the ghost.

Chapter Twenty-Nine

As soon as Martin had closed the door behind him, they were up and running. They leaped to their feet and raced towards the house. Billie had never run so fast in her entire life, and she had never been so angry. How dare Martin ruin things for other people? She was so furious that the fear that caused the pain in her tummy earlier on completely disappeared.

They hadn't thought through this part of the plan very carefully, which immediately became obvious. They had simply decided that they would go into the house and catch the ghost red-handed. But as they thundered up the steps and onto the patio, Billie wondered whether that would be enough. Why should Martin be afraid of three kids?

But he *was* afraid. That was very clear. Simona yanked open the door and went in first. Aladdin and Billie were right behind her, and none of them made any attempt to be quiet or cautious.

'Stop right there!' Simona shouted when they found Martin in the spare room clutching a cardboard box.

He looked terrified, and dropped the box with a crash. Then he simply stood there staring at them, but by then his expression was neither frightened nor angry. He just looked sad. When Billie looked him in the eye, she saw so much sorrow that she felt like crying.

On the little table with the coloured tiles lay another of the drawings that Billie had put away on the very first day when she and her mum moved in. Billie went over and read the words on the drawing.

Final warning.
If you don't stop searching right now,
it's all over.

'Did you write this?' she said crossly, pointing at the drawing.

It looked as if a child had formed the letters, but Billie didn't think that was the case.

'Yes,' Martin said quietly. 'It was me.'

Billie's anger was mixed with pity. What was Martin up to? And why?

'And is it you who's been sneaking in here and messing with things? Is it you who's been tapping on the windows at night?'

Martin nodded, and a solitary tear trickled down his cheek. Billie swallowed hard to stop herself from crying too.

'You have to understand . . .' Martin began. 'I

wanted . . . I wished . . . I . . .' His voice disappeared in a sigh.

'What?' Aladdin said, stepping into the room. 'What is it that Billie has to understand?'

Martin took a deep breath. 'I just didn't want anything bad to happen to you and your mum. The way something bad happened to me once upon a time.'

Billie shook her head. 'You didn't want anything bad to happen to us? How does that work? You did everything in your power to make me hate this house. And bad things have happened to everyone who lived here before me and Mum. Everyone. Someone's stove even caught fire. I suppose you were behind all that as well?'

'No,' Martin said. 'No, I've never hurt anyone. Not like that. The business with the stove must have been an ordinary accident. I just wanted the house to stand empty. Because that's what they want. The glass children. No one can escape them. Sooner or later, it will all end badly. For everyone.'

It was Simona who suggested they should go and sit in the living room. Martin sank wearily into the armchair that had once belonged to Billie's dad; it was one of the few pieces of furniture they had brought with them from town.

'I'm not sure how much you already know,' Martin said. 'But I used to live in this house with my mother and father.'

'We know all about that,' Aladdin broke in. 'We've spoken to your father.'

Martin's mouth dropped open. 'You've spoken to Manne?' he said in astonishment.

Billie nodded proudly. When she thought about it, they'd spoken to quite a few people.

'In that case you must know a lot already,' Martin said quietly. He patted one leg of his trousers, as if he could see a crease that needed smoothing out.

And then he began to talk.

* * *

'I was five years old when the house caught fire and my mother died. The police said it was an accident, but when I was older I found out about the history of this house. It had been a children's home where some of the children had died, and a nurse had hanged herself in the living room.'

Martin paused for a moment and glanced up at the light that Billie and her mum had put up.

'Our light used to swing to and fro,' he said in a shaky voice. 'Even though the doors and windows were closed. It happened several times. I don't remember anything else, but that's enough. This house is haunted by the dead who cannot rest in peace. They don't want anyone else to live here. They punish those who stay. That was why they burned down our house.'

He fell silent once more and looked at Billie.

'That's why I've been coming here and doing all those things – so that no one will want to stay here long enough for something serious to happen. For someone to die.'

'You're lying,' Billie said. 'You're the one who's been making the light swing to and fro. You're the only ghost in this house.'

'Besides, serious things have happened here,' Aladdin said, sounding quite angry. 'Take the family who lived here before Billie, for example. The little girl nearly drowned!'

Billie suddenly had a horrible suspicion. 'Was it you who tried to drown her?' she said, hardly able to make herself look at Martin.

He looked as if he might start crying again. 'They'd been living here for such a long time,' he whispered. 'And they'd moved out all the furniture. It was only the little girl who thought the place was haunted, and that wasn't enough. Something really terrible had to happen in order to convince them. I swam underwater when she was playing on her own. I pulled her down and held onto her. I would never have killed her. Never. And she wasn't hurt, just frightened.'

Simona tucked her legs under her on the sofa.

'You're crazy,' she said. 'You've upset people to make them move out. You just can't do that kind of thing.'

'But I've succeeded,' Martin said loudly, suddenly sounding angry. 'No one has died since my mother burned to death here! Not one person!'

No one spoke. Billie didn't know what to say. She couldn't find the right words for what she thought Martin needed to hear.

'You think this house is full of dangerous ghosts? For real?' Aladdin said eventually.

'I don't *think*. I *know*.'

'But the fire that killed your mother was an accident.'

'It most certainly was not!'

'And that's why you've persecuted everyone who's moved in here?'

'Yes.'

'But why did you rebuild the house in the first place?' Billie said. 'If you already knew there was something wrong with it, why did you restore it?'

'Because I had to,' Martin said. 'Don't you understand? If the glass children didn't get back their home, they would never leave me in peace. When my father bought the house, a lot of furniture from the children's home was still here. He cleared out the lot, and repainted the whole place inside and out. I think that was his biggest mistake, trying to get rid of all the old stuff, as it were. Before we moved in, the ghosts had been left in peace. When I renovated the house, I made sure everything was just as it had been from the start. To keep the children happy.'

His strange story made Billie's head spin. She didn't think there was much point in talking to Martin any more. It was just as his father had said: he had been damaged by what had happened when he was a child. Sad but true. However, there was one more question she had to ask:

'If you thought the house was so dangerous,

why didn't you leave it empty? Why did you sell it?'

Aladdin and Simona nodded in agreement. They were wondering exactly the same thing.

'Because I needed the money,' Martin said with a sigh. 'I had no choice. The bank was after me. My fishing business was going downhill. If I didn't sell the house, I would end up homeless. I wasn't living here myself; I had another house. And it just got too expensive. I couldn't possibly move in here, of course, but I have always seen this house as my responsibility. Whenever a family has moved out, I've come along and sorted everything out before the next family moved in. I've always tried to be a support for those who have lived here, and made sure that they escaped in time. Before the glass children came after them.'

He leaned back in the armchair. 'You can say what you like, but I know I've done the right thing. The responsible thing.'

Billie thought that Manne had probably been right when he said that Martin went a bit funny on the night when his mother died. Everything he said was so odd. To think that he had spent his whole life chasing ghosts that didn't exist.

'Tell me how you made the light swing,' she demanded.

Martin shook his head. 'I've already told you,' he said. 'It moves by itself. I swear!'

Billie looked at Aladdin and Simona. They shook their heads. Martin was lying. Obviously he was the one who had made the light swing to and fro on its hook. Somehow.

'So what about the handprint in the dust?' Billie said. 'I suppose that wasn't you either.'

'That was me,' Martin said. 'I sneaked in when you and your mum had gone off on your bikes and made a little print using a doll's hand. And I climbed up a stepladder to tap on the windows.'

A doll's hand. And Billie had thought it was the hand of a small child.

'What are we going to do now?' Aladdin said.

Billie got to her feet. 'I'm going to call Josef,' she said.

She turned to Martin and said firmly: 'You stay here.'

'Of course,' he whispered. 'Where else would I go?'

Chapter Thirty

The leaves lying on the ground looked as if they were on fire. Red and yellow and brown. Billie thought they were beautiful, and trod on them as gently as possible as she carried the last box to the trailer Josef had borrowed from a friend.

'So now we're just waiting for your mum,' Josef said when they had added the box to all the rest.

Billie breathed in the cold autumn air and squinted up at the sun, which for once had appeared in the sky.

'Is everything OK now?' Josef asked.

Billie thought about it. Yes, everything was OK.

'Good,' Josef said. 'But you still want to carry on going to school here in town?'

'This is where all my friends are,' Billie said.

'What about Aladdin?'

'I see him all the time anyway.'

Billie's mum emerged from the house.

'It's a bit sad, isn't it?' she said once they were in the car.

Billie looked at the house one last time. Several weeks had passed since she, Simona and Aladdin had unmasked Martin as the ghost. Her mum was better now, and with Josef's help, Billie had told her everything that had happened. Mum hadn't been able to apologize enough for not believing Billie when she had tried to tell her what had been going on in the house at night.

'You must have been so frightened,' she said over and over again, hugging Billie as tightly as she could.

Billie didn't try to stop her. Because she had been frightened. Almost all the time.

Josef had arrived less than twenty minutes after Billie called him that day. He wasn't alone; he had another police officer with him. They listened as Billie and her friends explained what they had done and what they had found out, then they took Martin off to the police station in town. Later Josef told Billie that Martin had told them everything; a lot of the things he had done were illegal, so he would probably end up being punished in some way.

Of course it wasn't exactly news that you couldn't go around doing what Martin had done, but Billie couldn't help feeling a bit sorry for him.

'I really believe he thought he was doing the right thing,' she said to Josef.

'I agree,' Josef said. 'But unfortunately that doesn't make it less illegal or less wrong. What if that little girl had drowned, for example? That would have been terrible.'

When it was all over and Billie's mum was back home, Billie and Aladdin had cycled over to see Ella and to tell her what had happened. She had sat and listened in silence.

'I was so sure the house was actually haunted,' she said when they had finished.

'But it wasn't,' Billie said firmly. 'It was just Martin, doing a load of weird stuff.'

When Mum was completely better, she and Billie had had a long talk about what to do with both their houses. Mum had said that she would really like to carry on living in Åhus.

'I know it's been hard for you,' she said to Billie. 'But I still think it would be better for us if we didn't stay in the house in town. There are so many sad memories there. Lots of good ones too, of course, and we will bring those with us. But I'd like to leave the rest behind. What do you think?'

Billie thought it over for a long time, and eventually she said that she would agree to move to Åhus, but on two conditions.

'Whatever you say,' Mum said with a big smile.

First of all, Billie wanted to stay on at her school in Kristianstad. And secondly she wanted them to get rid of all the old furniture from the children's home, and bring their furniture from town. Mum immediately agreed on both counts.

And now they were sitting in the car with everything packed in the trailer, heading for Åhus. Their new home.

She had asked her mum about Josef. Were he and Mum together, and would he be moving in with them?

Her mum had said: 'Josef and I are just friends. We'll see what happens in the future. He might become more than a friend, and he might not.'

Aladdin was sitting waiting on the steps when they pulled onto the drive. He waved, grinning from ear to ear as he ran towards the car.

'Food from Mum and Dad,' he said to Billie's mum, handing her a plastic carrier bag.

'Thank you, that's so kind!' Mum laughed.

Aladdin and Billie carried the boxes that were to go up to Billie's room, while Mum and Josef carried the rest.

The house was transformed. They had got rid of all the old furniture, and repainted the walls and ceilings. It was much lighter and more homely. On the outside the walls were still patchy, but the paint had stopped falling off. A painter had been to have a look.

'I should think the paint has been flaking off because the surface wasn't prepared properly when it was redone,' he said. 'If you just paint on top of the old stuff, there's always a chance that it won't take.'

So that was that. Mum had decided that they would have the outside of the house repainted next spring.

Billie started unpacking while Aladdin sat on her bed, flicking through a magazine.

'Your dad was pretty stylish,' he said, looking at a photograph Billie had placed on her bedside table.

Billie laughed. It was just typical of Aladdin to use a word like stylish.

Mum called up the stairs: 'Billie, can you come here for a minute? I want to know if you think the pictures we got from Grandma and Grandpa look OK in the spare room.'

'Coming!' Billie shouted, running downstairs.

She could hear Josef and Mum talking in the spare room, and headed in that direction.

And that was when it happened.

As she walked past the living room, she stiffened. Had she really seen what she thought she had seen, or was it just her imagination? And did she want to know the answer?

But it was already too late.

Slowly she turned round and looked into the

room where she had sat with Simona, Aladdin and Martin. She hadn't been imagining things.

The ceiling light was slowly swinging to and fro.

As if someone was hanging from it.

ABOUT THE AUTHOR

Kristina Ohlsson is a political scientist, with recent experience as a Counter-Terrorism Officer. She has previously worked at the Swedish Security Service, the Ministry for Foreign Affairs and the Swedish National Defense College. *The Glass Children* is her first novel for children and has been a prize-winning bestseller in Sweden.

Kristina lives in Stockholm and is now a full-time writer.

Growing up in a lonely mansion with her
fiercely strict father, Charity Delafield is
forbidden to explore, to set foot beyond the
iron gates – even to read fairy tales. No one
will tell her why.

But Charity has a secret.

All her life, she has been haunted by a dream
of a strange, hidden room, deep within
the house. One wintry day, she makes a
breathtaking discovery and begins to unravel
the enchanting, tragic, magical story that has
been kept from her for so long.

'Deliciously eerie' Daily Telegraph

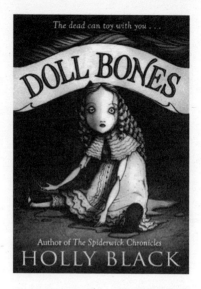

The dead can toy with you . . .

DOLL BONES

Author of *The Spiderwick Chronicles*

HOLLY BLACK

My name is Eleanor Kerchner.
You can call me the Queen.
I died in 1895.
Now it's time to play.

A chilling ghost story from the bestselling
author of the *Spiderwick Chronicles*.

The little car that won a war . . .

The Tin Snail

CAMERON MCALLISTER

Thirteen-year-old Angelo knows there's
only one thing that can save his father's job:
inventing a car the world has never seen
before. But it won't be easy – especially when
war is declared and he finds out the Nazis are
planning to steal his design!

Move aside Chitty Chitty Bang Bang; meet the
Tin Snail! Discover the extraordinary story –
inspired by real events – of how one little car
helped to win a war.

Here are six magical stories to thrill and enchant you. Watch Blackberry Blue rise from the bramble patch; follow Emeka the Pathfinder on his mission to save a lost king; join Princess Desire as she gallops across the Milky Way on her jet-black horse.

These beautifully written and original stories will delight readers of all ages, and the stunning illustrations by Richard Collingridge will take your breath away.